64/148

88

155

The Last Night on Bikini

The Last Night on Bikini

Patricia MacInnes

William Morrow
and Company, Inc.
New York

Grateful acknowledgment is made to the following publications, in which parts of the book originally appeared in earlier versions:

Chicago: *"View from Kwaj"*; The Chicago Tribune: *"Angle of Incidence"*; The New Generation: *"View from Kwaj"*; Seventeen: *"Swear"* (appeared as *"The Tunnel"*) and *"View from Kwaj"*; Shankpainter: *"The Last Night on Bikini"* (appeared as *"Bikini on Film"*) and *"Maybe a Wave."*

It is the policy of William Morrow and Company, Inc., and its imprints and affiliates, recognizing the importance of preserving what has been written, to print the books we publish on acid-free paper, and we exert our best efforts to that end.

Library of Congress Cataloging-in-Publication Data

MacInnes, Patricia.
    The last night on Bikini / by Patricia MacInnes.
        p.   cm.
    ISBN 0-688-08001-4
    I. Title.
    PS3563.A31168V5   1995
    813'.54—dc20   94-17929
                                              CIP

Printed in the United States of America

First Edition

1   2   3   4   5   6   7   8   9   10

BOOK DESIGN BY LINEY LI

For my mother, Ruth,

and brother Bill—

with love, profound

admiration, and in honor

of their work, humor,

and love across the

territories

*This book is a work
of fiction, based on
historical fact. Some
Pacific nuclear testing
incidents portrayed
are drawn from events
that occurred during
the testing in the States.*

ACKNOWLEDGMENTS

My deepest gratitude to the following people:

James Landis for the opportunity and support. Glenn Alcalay—political activist, medical anthropologist, and cultural tour guide—for his hard-earned expertise in the Marshalls and generosity in allowing me to tag along with him. Carl Clatterbuck, story doc and writing mentor. Rita Funk-Hoffman, who designed the cover. Dale Dyer, who did the illustration. Randy Hoffman for his photography. Tom McNeal for his editorial direction. Mary Allen, who provided suggestions and support. My brother Tim and father, William, for their assistance and knowledge. The people of Utirik for their warmth and hospitality. Mary Jack Wald—my diligent agent, Juanita Wilson, Caroline Patterson, Fred Haefele, Bob Shuman, Joyce Engelson, Judy and Greg Ervice, Greta Berg, Ehud Havazelet, Michael West, Katherine and Steve Hon, Steven Leveen and Levenger, Jim Mack, and Ron Jennings.

For the gifts of time and/or money, my grateful appreciation to The Ludwig Vogelstein Foundation, Stanford University and the Wallace Stegner Fellowship Program, Lee and Brena Freeman and the *Chicago Tribune*, Provincetown Fine Arts Work Center and the Zimtbaum Foundation, the California Arts Council, The MacDowell Colony, Ragdale Foundation, Virginia Center for the Creative Arts, Montalvo Center for the Arts, Blue Mountain Center, and Cummington Community of the Arts.

CONTENTS

History may be servitude,

History may be freedom. See, now they vanish,

The faces and places, with the self which, as it could, loved them,

To become renewed, transfigured, in another pattern.

—T. S. Eliot

The Last Night on Bikini

The Last Night on Bikini

The notion to take us to Bikini for the first atomic test in the Pacific came to my father, Jack, in a flash of sloe gin inspiration at the officers' club. It was 1946, Kwajalein Island in the war-wrecked Marshalls, a mound of mud and burst shell turned atomic frontier boomtown, 175 miles from ground zero Bikini. In four months the sound of the bomb would crackle live on radio back in the States. Jack foamed up two shot glasses with beer for my brother, Bubba, and me to toast that night in Com-Closed, the commissioned officers' club housed in a Quonset hut, and then he called us pioneers.

When I called us lucky, my father made that my nickname, and it would stick more than LeeAnn for the next decade. I was nine, and Bubba was a year older, the only kids on the island. My old man had pushed the limit bringing his family out; then he pushed it further. We'd just returned from Bikini, where we had been witness to the native evacuation. My father wanted us to be part of history and had hopes we'd show up in all the newsreels. He even made his own films with a new Bell & Howell home movie camera.

In the club Jack was shooting his angled, unsteady movies—dark bar shots of the wing end from a Wildcat fighter
on the wall, photos of dead aces, and some looped Navy
nurse on a bet unhooking garters from the shadowed tops
of her rayon stockings, smearing a stocking over stubble on
a lieutenant's jaw.

Bubba was trying to read a book at the table. He'd been
depressed ever since his ant farm had broken open during
shipping from the States. The box arrived with ants crawling
over it, most of the colony lost. Bubba could block out anything, he'd tell me when we got older, including military life
and the family he was in, if he had some junky science fiction
to read.

My old man called him Bubble Eyes or Bubba for short
because he read constantly. Sometimes Jack called him Oppie
for Oppenheimer. He had hopes that Bubba might help build
an even bigger bomb one day. My brother's real name was
Jim, and he thought Bubba was an asinine name, but somehow it persisted.

Jack was going on about bringing Bubba and me to
Bikini on Able Day to watch the fireworks from one of the
observation ships, although my father wasn't even involved
in the testing. He was one of the administrators for the dispen-
sary and later the hospital that would be built.

"Bomb's the biggest shoot-the-shoots you'll ever see,
and you kids are going to be in the motion picture." The
movie was a big-bucks Hollywood-type production the military was preparing to do about America in the atomic age.

"Like being in *Gone With the Wind*," Jack said. "Who
knows? Your friends in the States could see you in the mati-
nees, members of Operation Crossroads, living history, not
just reading about it. You'd think you'd end up in at least

one shot." Bubba made a face. He hated being photographed, but he closed his book.

"Hell, yes." Jack got louder. "And seeing the blast could earn Bubba his Webelos badge. I'll have to get a word with that goddamn Spike."

Spike was the vice admiral, and my father talked as if he knew him. It was always goddamn Spike this or that. I'd only seen goddamn Spike in a magazine photo. He and his wife were cutting into an angel food cake in the shape of a mushroom cloud. I knew Spike was predicting thousand-mile-per-hour winds at ground zero and temperatures as blazing as the sun's surface.

"Is You Is, or Is You Ain't My Baby" came on the jukebox, and my father started singing it to us. Bubba turned away from him, embarrassed, and went back to reading. Jack wasn't usually this merry, but it was history he loved and our fascination with it that made him gabby. He liked to recite the major battles of World Wars I and II and the Civil War, the strategies, and number of casualties. In the States we'd hunt together for Minié balls on Civil War battlefields, Indian arrowpoints, even old whiskey bottles turning violet in the sun.

Jack was still singing when the Lone Ranger came in: Joe Beebe, an Army Air Force pilot. Beebe was wearing a Lone Ranger mask and a Dodger cap like he'd do sometimes. His hair was chopped in a Mohawk, the initiation rite as a shellback when he flew over the equator recently to the Gilberts. A buddy with him had on a red-checked tablecloth over his head like an Arabian headdress. Someone clanged the bell strung up over the bar, recognition that fighter pilots had entered. "So we'll kiss their butts," Jack always said.

Coming into the club dressed like that was just for the

hell of it, out of boredom, but it always pissed off my old man. He thought they were being smart-asses in the getup.

The first time I saw the Ranger I knew there was something right about his wearing the mask, even before my old man told us he was one of the B-29 fliers detailed to track the cloud after the atomic blast.

I was in love with the Lone Ranger on the radio and a picture on a jigsaw puzzle box. His face was in two blurry puzzle pieces, but the box got to me. He was dressed in a powder blue cowboy suit, his hat shadowing the black mask. Silver, his horse, was rearing up out of a book, "the pages of history," but the Lone Ranger was in perfect control. Joe Beebe was like that. I was nine, but I was in love with him in some confusing way that I didn't understand. And whatever riptide effect I'd finally have on him wouldn't arrive for eight more years.

"Kid was a P-38 pilot. Shot down over the Philippines." The way my old man talked about Joe Beebe in such a clipped and deliberate way, I had the sense that the war was still on, and he was relaying immediate combat dope over a walkie-talkie.

"His wingman, best buddy, was killed in that flight." I'd heard Jack talk about the crapshoot in combat and the guilt for surviving. During the war Jack had switched places at mess with a left-handed guy on some base, and minutes later the southpaw got hit with machine-gun fire. "Christ, why that shipmate, why not me? The guy was even saying grace," Jack had said. "That's the thanks he got."

My old man went on about the Lone Ranger. "Can't be more than twenty-two and he's been decorated like a goddamn Christmas tree. Flying Cross, Purple Heart, every other goddamned thing." I knew Jack wanted the Purple Heart, even at the price he would have had to pay.

The Ranger walked with a limp for the Heart. The effort to move his right leg forward came from his hip and took the pull of his body. His leg acted as if it wanted to be left behind.

My father thought most fighter pilots were cocky and full of shit, but he was also in awe of them. In Com-Closed there were always stories like the one about the ace who played chicken with a Zero so close they grazed each other and Jap paint had to be buffed from his wing.

"You know what Beebe's baseball cap means, don't you?" Jack didn't pause before cluing us in. "Teams passed out caps for every Jap fighter they got. Eh, the Brooklyn Dodgers no less. Even Dem Bums got in on the act."

"To Be Specific, It's Our Pacific," an old war tune, started to play, and Jack stood up with the camera. He set off across the wood-plank floor, doing the rumba and filming the Lone Ranger as he bumped by his table. Bubba and I left the bar as if we didn't know our father.

My old man had spent his war bonus check on the camera and reams of film. The Bell & Howell had duct tape holding together the casing that had cracked open when my mother, Matty, whacked the camera out of his hands the night we flew into Kwaj.

Matty had been steaming in a green wool suit and white gloves, an outfit that made me think of asparagus tipped in mayonnaise. "That son of a bitch," she'd said with her back hills Ozarks accent as we stepped off the plane. Jack hadn't shown up to meet us. "I suspicion he got liquored up. Got hit over his head, is lying dead somewhere, and someone run off with his check." Matter-of-fact catastrophic thinking was always a way of life.

My father arrived an hour later with the camera and stumbled by us drunk to shoot the C-54 we came in on. My mother left her opinion of that on the Bell & Howell. The movie camera bounced once when it hit the ground. On the film that was salvageable, a white glove is exploding into the frame.

Bubba had gone behind the plane to throw up at the thought of what life here was going to be like. Outside in the night that first time, I could hear the ocean thrumming the reef.

The first night on Kwaj and now this one, as we came out of Com-Closed, the tropical air was weighty, salt so heavy it would short out Geiger counters later. Bubba and I walked back from the bar through mud that held the battles— tank tracks, rusting gears of artillery, Japanese soldiers still layered in the bombed tunnels. Every spark of star could be seen in the sky converging to ocean, to the lit barracks and Quonset huts that followed the crescent sweep of the island, to one Quonset hut where the atomic bomb would be assembled. This night, more than ever before, I understood that I'd always have peculiar things, freak things. I would never have what other people have. I began believing I was different, and my life would always be different.

Those months before the testing, I wandered around Kwaj. I hunted for war relics: machine-gun shells, shards of Japanese beer bottles, shrapnel. An area a little over one square mile and every foot of it had been hammered with one hundred pounds of steel during Operation Flintlock.

For almost four years we'd lived in fear of the Japanese. We'd waited with barrage balloons, Mickey Mouse gas masks, blackout curtains, even a blackout patch for the bright lime-colored dial on the radio.

But the war was over. We were living on a victory battlefield now, on top of the dead enemy. "Slap the Jap

Right Off the Map" had just come off the jukebox in Com-Closed. We'd proved it. Soon we'd be living with the gadget that did it.

Every day I walked the perimeters of Kwaj, watching for Gilda and the Manhattan scientists. I heard Jack first talk about it in Com-Closed with Louie Tucker, a warrant officer like my father.

At first when Louie and my old man talked about Gilda, I thought Rita Hayworth or her new movie *Gilda* was coming to Kwaj. But Louie said Gilda would have blown another thirteen-kiloton kiss to the Japs if they hadn't surrendered, and I got it.

I asked each day if she'd arrived. I never knew when it was going to happen. "Ten years in the brig for yapping about classified dope," Jack said, as if I were going to pass on secrets to the Russian subs parked in the waters around the island.

Besides watching for Gilda, I looked for the Lone Ranger's plane taking off from the airstrip, circling the lagoon, and then flying on for maneuvers.

The inevitable was coming, and we all prepared for it as if it had been the war effort. My mother was making Army uniforms for the pigs that would be boarded on the target ships set up to be bombed. Each day I'd wake to the whir of Matty's sewing machine as she worked over the little uniforms of no-flash material, detailing them with drawstrings and zippers just like those on GI field jackets. The military was experimenting with clothing on pigs because their hides were the closest match to human skin.

"Son of a bitch, they're training those pigs to stand up," Jack told us. "Going to shave the swine, coat them in suntan lotion, and they'll rise to attention in uniform at H hour, by God."

Matty made little rank stripes for the shoulders of the pig uniforms, from private E-1 all the way up to general. I'd help whipstitch them on. My mother sewed clothes for my brother and me also, durable enough to withstand an atomic bomb. She didn't believe in frilly outfits for girls. If she'd had any extra no-flash material, I would have had a dress.

When the pig trainer and his white Chester pigs arrived on Kwaj, Bubba and I went to the corral to see where the uniforms were going to end up.

"The bacon breaker, the pork master" people had started calling the trainer, even before he'd arrived. He was a ruddy-faced, surly man. Using crackers, he'd try to tempt the pigs so they'd sit up like dogs. But the pigs ignored him. They'd run over to us, and the breaker would yell that we were disrupting training. By eleven each day the bacon breaker was in a dark corner at Com-Closed drinking rum.

I'd stop to see the pigs a few times every day. Sometimes I'd limp around like Joe Beebe and then go over to the shed where he worked during his off hours. I'd heard he was building an outrigger like the kind the Bikinians used. People kidded him that he'd turned native since visiting Bikini. Beebe had been on the island at the same time as we were for the evacuation.

I had my own souvenirs from Bikini, the natives' abandoned possessions that I'd brought back to Kwaj: a fan, a scrap of fishing net, a belt woven from pandanus. I kept them with my other relics.

One day on Kwaj I walked into the shed where Joe Beebe was working on the outrigger. I was dragging my leg the way he did, as if it were a water witching stick divining to the ground. Coral dust spun up around me. Beebe had a breadfruit tree trunk set up on wooden sawhorses and was chopping out the fibery core with an adz. The wood was a butter color. In a corner was a bucket of salt water with a stringy tangle of soaking coconut husks. I'd seen Marshallese men pound the fibers to use for rope.

The Lone Ranger didn't look up from his work on the boat, even when he knocked over his half-lit cigar. I watched from the doorway, never speaking. I thought fighter pilots were unreachable, a breed apart. But that day I walked over to the cigar, picked it up, and put it to my mouth. Big hoot. I stood there waiting for him to look.

The Lone Ranger glanced up from the boat. His eyes were a sagebrush color. He was shirtless, and his skin was dark. "You smoke cigars, doll?" A southern accent, drawled out. I could have listened all day to the way he spoke. He laughed and then took the cigar from me.

Some nights I'd wake to the Lone Ranger's cigar smoke drifting into my room from his window just across the way. I wanted to know what kept him awake: guilt about his buddy's death or something else, if he was afraid. But Jack said fighter pilots didn't know fear. They wouldn't know fear if it were lava filling their mouths.

What I knew was that people in the States feared the Bikini test would trigger worldwide earthquakes and tidal waves, that it would split their skins like banana peels. A scientist predicted ships near ground zero would be swamped and there'd be no survivors. Even a Yale professor said the blast would crack the ocean floor and molten rock would spew in mile-high waves.

When anyone mentioned these points, my father always waved his hand in disgust as if he were pushing away bothersome flies. "Religious fanatics and ineffectual intellectuals."

I wouldn't tell my father or anyone that I was afraid.

The military said we were making history "for the good of mankind, to end all wars." I wanted to be a member of Operation Crossroads, a part of something important, to belong more than I ever had in any school or town we abandoned with each transfer.

To belong even if we had to die out here in this jumbled stratum of history, the nuclear age collapsing through war wreckage into "the Stone Age," how we described the natives' way of life.

I looked at the Lone Ranger reinventing the outrigger, concentrating on it as if he had nothing more on his mind. Without a sound I went over to touch the whittled wood.

The last night on Bikini, as I'd walked on the beach, I saw the Lone Ranger with a native girl in an outrigger. Newsreel cameras had filmed her earlier—May, an American fantasy of tropical bloom in paradise. Beebe was trying to teach her the words to "Good Night, Irene."

People in the village were asleep. May put her hand over the side of the boat, and I could hear her cup the water. It was that quiet.

The Lone Ranger made a slow outline over her mouth with red lipstick he'd given her that day.

I watched the boat rift the water and them together, not knowing what I watched. The water in what would become ground zero was already beginning to converge.

The day came when my father announced it. "She's here." Gilda had arrived on Kwaj.

Bubba and I had just walked into Com-Closed. We ran outside and looked toward the end of the island at a cluster of Quonset huts. Jack and Louie came out with their bourbons.

We stood watching the compound. Nothing looked any different.

"Fuck a bunch of motherfuckers," Louie kept saying, a line he often repeated.

"Can't we go see them put the bomb together?" Bubba said.

"I can't even get near the place," Jack said, chomping ice from his drink. "MPs got it guarded like bulldogs."

I'd heard that a blind girl 120 miles from the Alamogordo test site saw the flash. Acres of sand at ground zero had fused into creamy green glass, a Coke bottle–colored windowpane on the desert floor. I imagined Kwaj under glass like my brother's defunct ant farm, with us the colony ants living out our flat lives.

Bubba and I got ginger ales and went back outside. The drinks were too sweet, but we sipped them through red cocktail straws as we looked across the island at the junked tanks and gun emplacements, the churned mud and coral in small, stiff waves leading up to the Quonset hut.

"That Chick's Too Young to Fry" came on the jukebox, and Jack propped open the bar door. He talked Louie into dancing outside in front of the camera with Rita, a pet monkey, what the Navy called the Rita Hayworth pinup for the Army Air Force. Rita's hairy arms and legs wrapped around Louie's khaki shirt as he held on to the cup he spit Red Man chew into. She had on a little pair of turquoise polka-dotted underpants my mother had sewn, with a small cutout for her tail.

"Look, she's got enough religion for all of us," Louie said, flipping a cross on a thong around Rita's neck. He hummed along with the song, turned around to us, and laughed, crunching over the coral and dipping Rita as my father filmed them.

"Let's go tell your mother about Gilda," Jack said to us finally.

When we got to the house, Matty was in the kitchen. She'd just thrown a quart-size jar of pickles on a gecko, but it didn't die. She was on it with a skillet.

Jack held his arms out to keep Bubba and me back as if he didn't know what to expect from her. Matty was a force to be reckoned with and wasn't about to let lizards take over her house. She kept whacking at the gecko—dead now—as if it were a warning to other geckos. We stood and watched in amazement as she worked over the pickles and flattened lizard on the linoleum. A yellow tape measure from sewing hung around her neck like a streamer or ticker tape left after a celebration, and it flipped around as she struck with the heavy frying pan.

"It's just an old lizard," Matty said as I started to faint. I tried to focus on her oil painting on the walls. Since we came to Kwaj, she did winter landscapes, the snow thick as meringue on viridian Douglas firs.

Matty sat me in a chair, nudged my head down, and I put it between my legs.

"She's always so dramatic," Bubba said, waving a dish towel over me for effect.

Matty started cleaning up the mess, scraping up the smashed lizard with a spatula I'd never use again.

"The bomb's here," Bubba said. "But we can't see it."

"God help us we don't get blown to smithereens." Matty poured ammonia in a metal pail and ran water in it. "Breathe this," she told me, setting the bucket down by my feet. She went on with her clean-up, dunking the mop and slapping it over the floor.

"Spike might say we can go along to the fireworks," Bubba said.

"Spike? The vice admiral? You two just old shipmates?" She looked up at Jack as she wrung out the mop, dissolving a witch's brew of lizard blood and pickle juice. "You're not going out there, and they sure won't let kids."

"What do you know about it?" Jack said.

"I know those kids are not going out to see any damn atom bomb. We'll listen to it here on the radio."

"I thought we were going to see fireworks," Bubba said. "We're going to be in the movie."

"Look how you stirred them up over some crazy idea. Why do you do that?"

"No reason why we shouldn't be out there. Goddammit, why not?"

"Are you out of your mind?"

"You want to stop a chance of a lifetime? Something no other kids can even imagine. Front-row seats watching the test and being in the biggest movie ever made. You want to keep them from that?"

"I don't want to hear nonsense. Subject closed," Matty said, tossing the bucket of water out the door.

"So now she thinks she's goddamn Patton," Jack said, his voice raising. "Old Blood and Guts. Well, in case you're all interested, we're going to be there in the movie. Able Day, Mike hour. You better believe we're going to be there."

Reality was my father's invention. But I didn't realize that then. I expected to get an okay from Spike anytime for us to go out to ground zero.

That same day that Gilda arrived on Kwaj, I went to see the pigs. The sky was overcast; a tropical downpour was due. I'd brought caramels with me, and the flock gathered around as I held them out flat on my hand. I liked to watch the pigs work their mouths around the candy, but I couldn't stop thinking about where the animals were going.

Jack came out with the movie camera and some pig uniforms. He put his drink and camera down and climbed over the pen fence. Then he held one of the young pigs over the railing. "Suit it up," he told me. "Go ahead. Dress it like one of your dolls."

It was supposed to be a big joke. But seeing pigs dressed had lost something. Their skin was pale with albino white hair. As I held a pig, I studied the pores, the fine crisscross lines on the hide, and then the blond hairs and pores on my own arm.

Bubba showed up, and I handed the pig over to him. Bubba's being there made things less pathetic. He seemed irreverent about most everything. Without humor or grief, he dressed the pig in the general's uniform, tucking the front legs into the sleeves, zipping up around its taut sides as Jack filmed. It was starting to rain when Jack had us dress another one, a private. Drops sprang off the heavy white suit.

I held a caramel up to try to get them to stand. Jack wasn't through until we got the pigs upright. We stood in the rain, lifting their front trotters to mime salutes.

1 July 46, 0900. That was Able Day, H hour. If we were going to be vaporized, I wanted it to be announced, no time for fear. Maybe just a sudden mistake by the Manhattan scientists in the Quonset hut. As surprising as it was for the boy in Hiroshima who went out in his pajamas that August morning to see the squash fattening in his garden and never heard the pumpkin blossoms trumpet the most unlikely arrival.

They emptied the brig the night before Able Day and moved most of the people on Kwaj over to Ebeye, an island three miles away. Everyone remaining on Kwaj was outside, most of them drunk that early morning.

From my room I heard something explode. A loud bang and shattering, the splash of water. By the lagoon there was the sound of shouts. Right away I knew it was only a pipe or cherry bomb someone lit off in the water, but I held the bed and waited. At Hiroshima and Nagasaki, people were caught at the most mundane moments. A man clipping his fingernails, a woman sewing buttons on a dress, someone in the toilet. Someone writing a note, the fountain pen and his hand melted together.

It wasn't even dawn when Matty, Jack, Bubba, and I walked to the airstrip, hoping to glimpse Gilda loaded on board *Dave's Dream*. Jack said Rita Hayworth's picture had been painted on the bomb.

The reconnaissance B-29's were flying over as if it were an invasion, lights on their wings flashing. All night I'd smelled the Lone Ranger's cigar smoke until his kitchen door slammed as he left for the airstrip.

A crowd was gathering. It was a party on Kwaj, Mardi Gras. Sailors up on each other's shoulders in chicken fights, bottles of rye and gin passed around. Movie cameras. Radio equipment broadcasting to the States. MPs clustered around the crowd to keep us back from the landing strip and hangars.

My father's camera had gone back to Bikini without him. He'd passed it on to some sailor, who'd film the test shot for him from one of the observation ships.

At the far side of the airstrip a convoy of vehicles appeared, but we couldn't get near enough to see much. A radio announcer was reeling off every particular for broadcast when we noticed the jeep pulling a trailer. "There she blows," Jack yelled out as he focused his binoculars. "I bet you."

Gilda was beached under a white cover on the trailer. It didn't make sense that something that looked like nothing more than Christmas trees under a tarp had brought Japan to its knees.

The crowd went quiet as Gilda was winched up into the bomb bay in *Dave's Dream*. A large black *B* had been painted on the fin of the B-29. The propellers started up. With the five extra tons, *Dave's Dream* seemed too slow down the runway to pull up before the ocean at the end. The sailors behind us were rolling out shrill whistles.

"Will she make it?" the announcer said. "The world's fourth atomic bomb. Is *Dave's Dream* going to make it?"

The first thing I did back at home was set up the projector in the living room so I could watch the movies Jack had taken of Bikini four months before.

On film a dozen naked kids run by with spray guns of DDT shipped in to kill flies. Crates of K rations are opened, and teenagers tear into powdered lemonade that turns their mouths yellow. *Life* and *National Geographic* photographers are snapping pictures as islanders load mats and fishing nets into the LST.

Jack's hand appears, waving Bubba and me back in the crowd where a newsreel camera is filming. My yellow dress and the orange Mercurochrome on my legs, Bubba's Cub Scout uniform and his red hair all have turned out too brilliant on the home movie like the overdone dyes on postcards. We stand on the shore holding metal lunch boxes as if we're going off to a day at school.

Nearby are the Lone Ranger and the Bikini girl. Newsreel cameras film native women gathering around laughing as the girl twists the lipstick tube up and down. A frangipani blossom falls out of her hair.

That night my father filmed the natives coming aboard a Navy ship to see movies. A string of light bulbs illuminates the deck, and the Bikinians sit down on metal folding chairs. A military interpreter gestures by the projector, trying to explain to the islanders *Pardon My Past*, a Hollywood bedroom farce.

After the last movie the crowd watches the projector light on the screen in a night lit from a full moon. Native men glide into the lagoon in outriggers and spread out fishing nets one last time. They wave torches, slapping the water and yelling. Glimmering fish fly up in the nets. Torch flames scribble across the frames of black film.

My father's next shot shows a blaze riding the outriggers and village huts, ignited by the military the next day. You can't hear the loudspeakers on the beach blaring "I've Got a Gal in Kalamazoo" over the wailing islanders on the LST leaving for Rongerik. Two native men jump overboard and are swimming back to Bikini. That's where my father's film of the evacuation ends.

I stopped our home movie projector. Over the radio in the living room NBC was snapping out facts from a ship near the fleet of ninety-seven target ships. Forty-two thousand GIs waited nine to twenty miles from ground zero. Five-gallon gasoline drums, simulating human torsos, bobbed in the lagoon, ready to measure what damage could be done to a chest cavity. Punctured cans of condensed milk drifted in the water, set up to trace a creamy pattern of the radioactivity flow.

Thirty seconds to zero time. I went up to the roof where Jack, Matty, and Bubba were waiting, listening to the radio by the window.

On the observation ships, men were putting on dark goggles, six thousand handed out. The GIs that didn't get a pair covered their faces with their arms.

Twelve seconds and the countdown. Besides the pigs, there were goats, sheep, rats, even bedbugs on the target ships, waiting to rise.

When the radio announcer said, "Bomb away," we gripped the roof. Nothing. Thirty seconds to fall. "A flash like sheet lightning. A ball of fire," the announcer said. There was roaring in the background.

"Coils of smoke are lit up a salmon color. The mushroom cloud is now several miles across. It's climbing thirty thousand feet, forty thousand feet. The target vessels are obliterated by spray and mist. Everything has turned white."

Jack passed us the binoculars to try to make out clouds we couldn't see. "We almost got you two there," he said. "You kids could have been famous."

Bubba adjusted the focus on the binoculars. That day he had worn his Cub Scout uniform. The yellow scarf looked too big on him, almost like a shawl as the ends blew in his face.

We stayed on the roof waiting to see, but there was nothing. "That's all there is to the bomb?" Matty looked at us as if we'd know. "That's what the fuss was all about?"

At Bikini, automatic cameras on board the target ships were filming the pigs. At the instant of the burst the ranks were finally standing up as if at roll call.

Pilotless drone planes swept through the column. I knew the Lone Ranger was trailing the cloud, swatted into the outer ring of the shock wave. Special radiation meters on board the B-29 echoed gamma rays that beamed up in spokes from the target ships in the lagoon, tossed like an upset of bent knives and forks. Uniformed pigs gathered behind the ships' portholes, their eyes glazed behind sandy eyelashes.

Emblazoned on the general was the imprint of the private finally standing straight up, his mouth gaped in a squeal of terror and his trotters stretched to their cloven limits, as if he, Private E-1 Pig, could hold back the splitting of atoms.

People called the bomb drop a dud, a flop, Operation Chloroform.

"Screw them. What do they know?" Jack said. "We're still totaling the damages. Besides, we've got Baker test, an underwater blast, in three weeks. It's just the beginning."

The military's movie about the atomic age would never

be completed. Maybe it was the disappointing fireworks or the fact that some GIs were already starting to show effects of the radiation.

After the blast I got out my box of souvenirs from Bikini and relics from the States. I slivered off some of my hair with an Indian point and a piece of coral from Bikini. My hairdo wasn't a Mohawk, but I was a shellback. It was initiation, the beginning of the testing, the first time over the equator. Even though we were nine degrees north of zero, we'd crossed over. In a different hemisphere, water swirls counterclockwise, lagoons funnel upward. We were governed by a different set of rules now.

The sailor who filmed Bikini with my father's camera brought back some dark goggles and a beer bottle of Bikini sand as mementos from Able and gave them to Jack. Reels of the film were developed, and my father ran movies of the blast almost day and night in the living room, even when no one was there. The atomic cloud looks like cauliflower rising in the sky.

The sailor had filmed Bikini Lagoon when his ship sailed back a few hours after the blast. There are jerky shots of a reporter in shorts typing a story on the red bull's-eye ship, the *Nevada*. The aft was only seared and pounded in. *Dave's Dream* had missed the ship by half a mile.

Only a few ships were sunk. Others near the bull's-eye had their decks exploded, superstructures torn apart. Sailors are playing shuffleboard on one of the undamaged cruisers. Some men on the ships are wearing jump suits and gloves like beekeepers. They hold up Geiger counters to a line of shirtless sailors in muscle poses.

On the Bikini shore GIs are playing volleyball, and some are swimming in the lagoon while the beekeepers wave Geiger counters over the beach to measure the hum.

An ensign grabs a woman's ass at the beer garden. Probably "I'm Beginning to See the Light" was playing over the loudspeakers as newsmen raise a toast and mouth the words.

In two years we'd see the evacuated Bikinians again when it was declared they were dying of malnutrition on Rongerik. Big green military tents and tables for a mess hall were set up for them in a camp at the end of Kwaj. I watched the islanders line up for dinner with military-issue plates in their hands.

The Lone Ranger was gone now, transferred out. The outrigger he finally completed had swamped in the Kwaj lagoon, short of Marshallese craft.

The Bikinians stayed on Kwaj for six months until it was decided what island they'd go to next. They had been asking for Bikini back ever since they were evacuated. "The children of Israel," what we told them they were when we took Bikini. "The children the Lord saved from their enemy and led into the Promised Land."

"Manhattan Transfers." That's what I'd heard the Bikinians called. Magazines and some of the brass would call the acquisition of Bikini for the testing the greatest PR job ever pulled off.

But on the natives' last night on Bikini all of us were singing "Good night, Irene, good night, Irene. I'll see you in my dreams." It was that time of expectation, of possibility, when great notions cover great lies. We believed then in a simplehearted undertaking of history.

On Bikini the movies were about to begin. The Bikinians were on deck in folding chairs, their kids on their laps. They held Dixie cups of warm Coca-Cola and small paper bags of popcorn. Joe Beebe cupped the hand of a boy with a red Yo-Yo and guided him through the flip of the wrist.

Everyone was damp in the humid night as they waited for motion pictures.

When the films started, some of the islanders got out of their seats. They came up to the screen to stop a steamroller from flattening Mickey Mouse, to lay their hands on Roy Rogers's silver-studded horse.

1952

Each base was an escape from the last. On moves in the States we'd fill the Oldsmobile to the top, Bubba's Miles Davis records warping in the back window, which just added another dimension to the music, Bubba said. Squeezed up front was a cooler filled with my father's beer on a block of ice for the drive.

I'd lie down on the floor in the back among boxes and suitcases and hold on to the velvety cord strung across the back of the front seat. Until I got carsick, I'd watch the telephone lines loop us from one base to another.

My family didn't take to moves well even though that's all we'd ever done. After Kwaj, we lived in San Diego and then China Lake, a base in the Mojave near where Chuck Yeager broke the sound barrier. In 1952 my father requested a second tour of duty on Kwaj.

Sixty-six test shots in the Marshalls from '46 to '58, ending with one called Fig. It was exactly because of the parade of bangs that my father wanted to be back. Nectar,

Yellowwood, Butternut, Romeo, Dogwood, Tobacco, Magnolia, Wahoo. I imagined an officer from the South at a gray metal desk, drowsy from a lunch of chicken-fried steak and a few beers at the officers' club, a fan ruffling papers around him as he conjured up names for the blasts.

During Operation Ivy in 1952 the first U.S. H-bomb vaporized Elugelab Island, near Eniwetok, and scooped out a canyon one mile across. "Crater Lake in the tropics" we called the phantom island. "Atlantis in the Pacific."

I was fifteen that year. The Korean War was going on, and in the States the race between Adlai Stevenson and Eisenhower was under way. But not on Kwaj. The island numbed in the tropical heat, cheap booze, and the magnitude of its mission.

Every day Bubba and I took Spam sandwiches out to the end of the island where garbage was dumped and the sharks circled.

"My life's in shreds; I welcome the plank," Bubba yelled. He stood on the end of a corroding World War II howitzer that stuck out over the water and pretended he'd jump off. Then we threw Spam out as far as we could to summon the fins.

Our mother had anticipated a state of emergency, afraid the nuclear tests might backfire. She bought up cans of Spam at the commissary in case there was ever food rationing and read up on recipes: Spam casseroles, omelets, Spam with pineapple. Matty always cooked the hell out of the Spam, like she did all meat. Growing up in the backwoods, she thought you had to burn out the worms.

"It's not squirrel, you know," Bubba told her one day in the kitchen. Matty glared up at him from a sputtering frying pan where slices of the pink slabs weren't even frying like regular meat. "Ground skunk, maybe," Bubba added.

My brother was an Adlai Stevenson supporter and made stenciled campaign flyers to put around the island. We thought up slogans like "Vote Smart—Vote Adlai" and "Take a Hike, Ike." Each day we'd have to repost the flyers. Someone was tearing down every one we'd put up. After feeding the sharks, we'd plaster more handbills on walls of the commissary, mess hall, church, and bars.

One day we stopped by the Snake Pit, the bachelors' bar, a concrete cave with a planter of fake bamboo foliage in the middle, like a duck hunting blind, and a bar fashioned from bamboo. A fan with large slow-moving wooden blades dominated the ceiling. Tacked up on a dartboard was the base commander's picture. Photos of nude women with pale skin covered the back wall. One pinup was holding a duck call to her lipstick-red mouth.

It was at the Snake Pit that I first noticed Dave Coyne, a loner I'd heard about who carried around a young owl he'd sneaked in from the States. "The General" he called it, a namesake for MacArthur and Eisenhower, my father had told us.

Over the General's eyes was a pattern of feathers that looked like a furrowed brow, as if the owl were scowling. Tufts on the bird's head stood up in horns, and the wing feathers were mottled brown like bark. The General looked around with glassy golden brown eyes the color of cologne in a clear bottle.

Strapped to Coyne's forearm was a wide leather band for protection from the bird's talons. Coyne held on to a little leash that could attach to leather strips around the owl's oversize claws, although his pet stayed on his arm without the restraint. At the bar Coyne had a bucket of small live fish for the General. The owl swallowed each one whole, turning his head in degrees as if he were mechanical.

There was something disturbing about Coyne, but I couldn't name it then. His dingy brown hair was waxy-looking as if he'd been the one to hatch. He had a tattoo on his pale upper arm, Betty Boop bending over bare ass in a short dress. The tattoo flashed from under the sleeve of his white T-shirt as he lifted fish to the General. Within a month Coyne would be shipped out for wounding a man, something I'd be there to see.

A sailor looking me over said something to Coyne, and Coyne said loudly, "No thanks, I like mine well done."

Bubba hung up the Adlai Stevenson flyer on one of the walls, and Coyne walked over, then took a minute to read the paper. The bird turned his head, blinking just one eye, and watched him. I remember thinking that Coyne was either contemplative, maybe even an Adlai fan, or just a poor reader because "Madly for Adlai" was all it said. Apparently that got to him. He ripped down the flyer, wadded it up, shoved it in his mouth, and chewed on it, poster paint and all, as he looked at me. "Guess I like Ike," he mumbled.

Some men at a table in the corner laughed. Coyne ran his eyes over me as if he were X-raying each detail and knew things about me that I wouldn't want anyone to know.

I gave an embarrassed laugh that I was mad at myself for later. Bubba turned around, and we left. "Another ignoramus for Ike," he said outside the bar.

As we headed home that night, I thought of Dave Coyne compressing a person down to hair and bone, like his owl might do, a pellet to be digested and brought back up later.

We were always isolated at new stations, transplants, outsiders. My family were hopeless social misfits. They didn't know how to be around people, and they didn't care. Bubba called everyone in the military a dolt or fathead. Drunk or sober, my father would rage anytime the phone rang or someone came to the door. "What the hell *you* want? Jesus Christ, goddamn son of a bitch, you picked the worst time."

My mother just didn't put up with gab. "I got work to do," she told talkative neighbors. "Time for you to go home."

On Kwaj there was no high school, although there were families on the island now and an elementary school. Bubba and I took a correspondence course and shipped out our homework every two weeks to the States.

I didn't want to be alone, but I didn't know how to be around people either. In San Diego I would go off with some boy into orange groves or the khaki-colored chaparral on the hillsides. Out in the Mojave we'd lie down on the scrubbed gravel of washes, the sound of sonic booms reckoning the desert air. We'd roll around with an urgency, far short of sex. Every time I thought I'd be changed. I was hopeful my life would be different. But nothing changed and the boys just seemed alike: their gestures, spearmint gum mouths, the feel of their slick backs, even what they said.

I never knew what to say to any of them. I'd get up from the bushes, where desert sand and twigs or eucalyptus pods branded cuneiform letters in our backs, and I'd act as if the boy wasn't there anymore. I'd wander away, on a search for something. In San Diego it was fossilized fish, whale bones in the limestone rocks near our house. In the desert I'd look for the prehistoric shrimp that came to life in the dried Mojave lakes when it rained.

Boys were never interested in a search for ancient creatures like I was, although in the Mojave Skip Watson caught a tarantula once and let it crawl up his arm. More often, though, the boys would comb their hair, tuck in their shirts, and act as awkward as I was. Sometimes I'd pretend I didn't even know them the next time I saw them.

I wanted to get lost in the desert, to become someone else or just invisible. On Kwaj it wasn't possible to get lost for long. But a few weeks after being there, I began taking walks around the island in the dark.

About midnight I'd crawl out my window. I'd walk by the generators to listen to the hum and then go along the oceanside to hear the waves. At night with everyone asleep it seemed like a different place. I imagined myself one of a handful of atomic holocaust survivors like in the movie *Five*. Or pursued by "The Thing from Another World," the radio-active vegetable from outer space.

Near the end of Kwaj was a Quonset hut I liked to go in. Bombs had been assembled there for the first tests, and an image of a bomb casing could still be seen on the cement floor. Workmen had painted the floor around the real vault, leaving the egg shape like a shadow falling over ground zero. A chalkboard for calculations still hung on a wall, and wooden office chairs were set around a table as if the Manhattan District were about to enter and commence work.

I'd stop by the Snake Pit and try to listen in to conversations. Usually all I heard was a low drone in the bar, an occasional outburst of swearing like machine-gun fire. I'd wait by the bar until after last call and the men stumbled out or were carried by buddies.

The night before Elugelab Island was blown up I saw Coyne wandering Kwaj also. I didn't know it was him at first, except for the General. Coyne had on a hooded sweat shirt pulled up on his head into an ominous point. He carried the owl on his arm.

I hid by a building so he wouldn't see me and watched as he walked around, pausing by Quonset huts and offices, trying the doors and glancing in the windows. When he came to one of our posters, he tore it down, clenched it into a ball, and stuck it in his zip-up sweat shirt.

Coyne stopped at one window where a couple was up with a crying baby, walking it back and forth in the room. From where I was, I could see the crib, the parents in bathrobes, a stuffed clown on a bureau. Coyne stood a few feet from the window and stared at the family. He held the bird up to his face, and then he did something I didn't expect. He suddenly rubbed his cheek against the owl's wing. He did it again, burying his nose in the smell of feathers. The tender gesture surprised me. I almost felt sorry for him.

I waited until he had walked on, and then I went back home that early morning. As I lay in bed, I imagined Coyne scrabbling around in the hibiscus outside. I got up and taped some of Bubba's Adlai flyers to the inside of the window, facing out. I papered over the whole pane.

The next day, November 1, we didn't know that an island had been obliterated. People in the States wouldn't know about it for another sixteen months until photos were declassified.

The number of islands in the Eniwetok Atoll had been reduced from forty-one to forty by way of the "humanitarian" bomb, the most economical form of destruction, *Look* would say. The bomb was no bigger than the average family living room, according to the magazine.

News of the lost island set off Matty. She'd read the government manual *You Can Survive* and decided we were going to have a bomb shelter outside our house. Jack called it a half-baked idea, but my mother got a shovel and began digging.

Matty had on black pants rolled up, a simple white cotton shirt, and a Chinese bamboo hat so she looked like a worker tending a rice field as she dug through the topsoil. Her hair strayed out from under the hat. She'd stop for a moment and wipe her forehead, then continue on.

"Jesus Christ, why don't you come in out of the sun?" my father yelled through the window at her.

My mother approached everything with a kind of frantic determination and commanding panic. Bubba and I were embarrassed at first and watched from the window or stood far enough away from the pit so that we wouldn't be recognized as her family. Later we went out and helped dig a little.

News about her bomb shelter spread, and by the second day people were coming to see it. They stopped and asked my mother for advice about defense structures.

When I spotted Coyne out front watching Matty dig, I froze where I was by the side of the house. The General was on his arm, and he was stroking the back of the bird's neck with a knuckle. Matty said something about his pet.

Coyne looked over at me suddenly and motioned with his head. "Your girl?" he asked.

"My daughter, Lee." Matty glanced at me. She was up to her neck in the pit.

Coyne had a smirk on his face. "I've seen her at night around the bachelors' bar, walking the island like she was, I don't know, looking for something. Girls got to be careful."

Matty glared in my direction. Then she threw a spade of dirt that almost hit Coyne. "Keep it moving, sailor."

Right away, before Matty even crawled out of the pit and got to the house to question me, I went inside and started devising a booby trap for Coyne. Later I got some wire and strung it at ankle level between shrubs and bushes outside my window. If he came back, I was ready.

No one went along that side of the house, but Bubba noticed the trip wires. "What's going on?" He laughed. "What are the mines all about?"

I had him paper over the outside of my window with the flyers to lure in Coyne. Then I tightened the wire more between the bushes.

News about the lost island made most people jumpier. But others played up the testing, maybe to deflect their fear. At the snack bar, chili dogs with everything on them were immediately renamed H-bombs. A bartender at Com-Closed invented the "bomb blast," a ring of ice in a tumbler with turquoise-colored gin and tonic to look like the Pacific, and a little flame added to set off everything.

When I lived in San Diego, there was a fourteen-foot plaster lemon in the middle of an outlying town. The lemon had even been in a parade float once. I wanted to live in a place where that was the town's monolithic symbol, not a living-room–size thermonuclear device.

The time between the island's disappearing and the presidential election was just four days. November 4 was the election in the States, but we were a day ahead on Kwaj, living in the tomorrow of the nuclear age on the other side of the international date line.

It was the day before the election on Kwaj that the explosion happened, a sound we'd been fearing. Bubba and I were posting flyers and were heading toward the commissary when a deadening explosion erupted. We looked around but couldn't see anything right then. Another blast rumbled.

I knew we were overreacting, but we immediately imagined the bomb testing out of control, or that the Korean War had heated up and the base had been attacked. Sometimes we heard rumors about what could happen on this strategic point in the Pacific. We were waiting for another explosion as we headed back to the house.

"What happened?" Matty yelled as she stood by the seven-foot pit waiting for us. She had on her Chinese hat. "Where the hell's your father?" Jack was nowhere around. By then we saw black smoke at the end of the island, rising above the palms.

Matty had already moved some cans of Spam and gallon root beer bottles of water down into the trench. More supplies were left at the top. "Get in," she ordered. "We're trying this thing out." Seconds later we heard fire trucks.

We stepped down a ladder and waded into six inches of water at the bottom of the hole. The cans of Spam were covered by the muddy water, and only the spouts of the water bottles stuck up. Bubba grabbed a shovel in the pit and started scraping mud and flipping it out of the trench. Matty and I scooped up water in metal buckets, and she emptied them at the top of the ladder.

Linda, a next-door neighbor, had just returned from the lagoon and was in the front yard when another detonation roared. The ground shook. Coral and topsoil fell in on us. "Get in," Matty yelled out at Linda. "Everybody get down."

Linda ran over to the bomb shelter and climbed down the ladder as we crouched at the bottom. She had on her beach robe, and her hair was in a bandanna around pin curls. "Who's bombing?"

"Us or the Russians. We'll have to keep our wits about us." Matty looked around the pit, which wasn't much bigger than a grave. "We're going to have to turn people away soon. I read about this."

A blast erupted again, and the ground trembled, sending in more dirt. We stayed hunched down at the bottom of the hole for the next fifteen minutes, waiting.

Matty finally stood up, holding the bucket in one hand, and in the other, the Chinese hat she was now using to bail. "Why the hell's the water coming up? I can't stop the god-damn water." Her voice was absorbed in the dirt walls.

Because Kwajalein was an atoll, the water was rising in through the coral. We'd never control this, although my mother believed she could control anything she set her mind to.

Matty reached deep in the dirty water for a can of Spam and opened it with the can key. Then, from a slot dug out in the trench wall, she pulled a kitchen knife she'd stored, sheathed in a cardboard holder. We all looked on, astonished. Matty cut thick, crooked slices of the Spam.

"There now, have something to eat," Matty said. "Enough for everyone." She speared the slabs, satisfied that she had planned efficiently to take care of her family.

We began debating whether to get the radio out of the house. A half hour later we were still talking about it when we heard Jack's voice.

We yelled out, and he walked over to the pit. "What the hell are you doing in there?" He peered in at us. "For Godsake."

"Is it safe?" my mother asked.

"Safe? What the hell you think is going on?"

Bubba gave a disgusted sigh and climbed out, not wait-ing for Jack's explanation about ammo detonated in some Quonset hut fire that day.

"Goddammit, you'd think it was the end of the world," my father roared.

"A fire?"

I thought there was disappointment in Matty's voice.

"Well, good God, I was sure we'd been hit."

That night before the election, Bubba and I went with Matty to the officers' club. We sat down at a table where Jack was bullshitting with the lieutenant commander, Ken Jennings. The commander started to rib my mother about her bomb shelter and what had happened.

"You got a swell shovel swing. The Army could hire you to dig trenches," he said as she sipped a glass of beer.

"More people ought to think ahead," Matty said. "You could order Geiger counters for everyone, too." She held the glass up to him.

"There's no risk to the base, ma'am." Jennings tapped a new pack of cigarettes against his wrist, peeled off the cellophane, and crumpled it.

"So did we intend to pulverize that little old island?" Matty always said what she wanted to in her unvarnished way.

"For Godsake, Matty." Jack lifted up from his chair as if it were on fire and leaned across the table to her. "You're talking to a lieutenant commander."

"Everything will be atomic energy one day," the commander said, lighting a cigarette and waving out the match. "Your kitchen toaster, stove. It's a matter of harnessing. Control." He punctuated it with his fingertips squeezed together on the match as if he held a pinpoint of plutonium on the end. "That's why we got the eggheads on board for this operation."

Matty seemed unimpressed as she wiped the table area around her with a cocktail napkin.

"Control," Jennings said again. "Just like anything else."

He put his hand over a round ashtray on the table and turned it as if he were twisting a dial. "I hear *The New York Times* put out a list of upcoming bomb blasts in Nevada for vacationers. We could show them something." He rolled out a long, fading whistle.

The commander got on to the election, and Bubba barked out the GOP slogan, "K-one, C-two: Korea, Communism, and Corruption."

"Knock it off," Jack mumbled to him. My brother kicked me under the table, and then he fled the club. I wasn't far behind him.

That night Bubba decided to do something more for Adlai. More campaigning to get out the word, he said, to make up for Coyne's tearing down the posters. I followed him back to the house, where he grabbed a few of his Davis, Brubeck, and Milt Jackson records. We went to the island radio station, just a small shack with a Kwaj-only broadcast run by a sailor who was always plastered. Bubba talked the DJ into taking the records in exchange for some airtime. Shortly after Bubba got in and they fooled around with the equipment, he ushered the guy out and locked the door.

I went over to the entrance of the Snake Pit to catch the broadcast. On loudspeakers at the bar I heard a needle scratch across "When I Fall in Love." Then came my brother's tentative voice.

It was a busy night at the club, and guys were sitting around, Coyne there with his owl. They'd gone quiet when Bubba came on, ad-libbing as he went. He called the Republican party the two-headed elephant, used Stevenson's line about talking up to people, not down, and then he went after McCarthy.

"Who the hell put him on?" someone said.

I was still standing near the entrance, trying to hear Bubba when Coyne noticed me and yelled out, "Get a load of this. What's she doing here?"

I didn't say anything and was about to leave, but he came up and blocked me. "You the entertainment?" he said. "How about dancing for us?"

I shook my head.

"You like to do that, don't you? Dancing in front of your window." He was close enough to me that I could smell whiskey and beer on his breath and a greasy odor on his striped shirt. The leather band around his forearm looked worn and filthy. The General cocked his head and spread one of his stately wings out a foot and a half. Everything seemed startling, exaggerated, wobbling loose.

"Come on," Coyne said to me.

"Leave her alone," a small guy at the bar mumbled.

"That your brother on the radio?" Coyne pushed his face in closer to mine. "The kid Communist?"

Over the speakers you could hear the sailor at the radio station beating on the door in the background, yelling, and trying to get back in. Then it sounded as if the door had broken open. Bubba was saying Stevenson's line about looking forward to great tomorrows.

The radio went dead. Music from my brother's warped "Dig" record came on along with the soused sailor garbling his words.

"You a Communist, too?" Coyne said to me. "Communist squirt?" His fleshy face looked almost contorted from the intensity of his words. There was a filmy look in his eyes.

"Fucking politicians. Ike and Adlai both stink," a sailor yelled out. "Eisenhower can go to hell. Who gives a shit?"

"Fuck you," Coyne said. "You don't talk about the next President that way."

"Free country, Coyne," the sailor shot back.

Coyne paused a minute like the time I saw him stop to read the poster. His doughy face suddenly looked flushed from the booze and the warm, sticky night. He stroked the back of the owl once and then grabbed his drink and walked over to the man who had yelled out about Eisenhower. "You a Red also?"

The sailor spit out some of the drink he'd just taken. "You're a real asshole, you know that?" he screamed. The sudden loud noise startled the General, and the owl shifted on Coyne's arm, raising his wings and clawing upright, hooking on to the armguard with his beak.

Coyne set his drink down and grabbed for the General, but the bird panicked more. The owl began beating his wings and making a contorted whoing that sounded as if he were part demon. A few down feathers drifted to the floor as the General took off from Coyne's arm and flew toward a wall. He hovered at the radio speaker a moment, tried landing, and then swooped across the room. The bar went quiet, waiting to see if the long wings would catch in the slow blades of the ceiling fan.

Coyne's face was in a grimace, his mouth opened, eyes wild. The General began circling the bar, the almost four-foot wingspan moving over the stunned men. We stared in amazement as if a pterodactyl had flown into the club. Coyne made a frantic dash below the bird, pushed some guy out of his chair, and stood up on the seat, waving his arms. But by then the owl had flown to the other side of the bar, issuing a watery dropping in mid-flight.

Coyne rubbed his thumbs together with his fingers to signal the General. Over the jazz I could hear the sound like soft grasses brushing together. "Baby," he called. "Baby." He ran to another chair, stood on it, and tried grabbing for the owl, but his frenetic movements only sent the bird flying in another direction, whacking once against a wooden fan blade.

Disoriented, the owl swooped back even closer to the paddles and caught in the turnstile. The fan halted, softly thumping the body of the bird. The owl screeched an almost human-sounding scream, and feathers sprayed. The paddle catapulted the bird across the room and to the floor. Coyne was riveted, horrified. No one else in the bar moved. The owl had one wing spread out and the other folded in against his body. The General was still for one moment, then began hobbling, stunned.

Coyne knocked over two chairs getting to his pet. With his beak open, the owl looked like he was panting.

"Damn if birdbrain isn't still alive." It was the sailor who'd had words with Coyne. "Someone ought to put it out of its misery and stuff it for a wall."

Coyne rose from his knees alongside the General. He moved smoothly without hesitation, almost a choreography, first grabbing the nearest bottle off a table and bringing it down on the table edge to crack off the bottom. Foam flew out, and pieces of the emerald glass tinkled, as delicately as wind chimes, when they hit the concrete floor. Coyne crunched on the glass as he stepped forward with the jagged edge. Without a word, he took a swipe, ripping open the man's uniform and slashing across his chest. A startling crimson suddenly blossomed on the sailor's white shirt. The man made a loud "guffaw" sound and bent over.

I'd heard war stories all my life, some about hand-to-hand combat. One time I asked a man what it was like at that moment. How easily, how softly a knife can go in, he'd said. It meets a man so unequivocally.

Coyne looked almost surprised at what he'd done. But

he held the bottle out in front of him, jiggling it in rage or fear. "Blue Tango" was playing in the bar now, and the drunk DJ was babbling on.

Within minutes MPs were at the Snake Pit, had Coyne handcuffed, and led him off. The wounded sailor was taken to the hospital.

"My bird," Coyne yelled. "I want my bird."

Later, after the General had recovered and the bands around his legs were removed, someone took him outside, and the bird lifted off.

I went back to the house. Bubba hadn't returned, and neither had my parents. I kept looking out my window, waiting for something, even though I knew Coyne was in the brig and probably would be shipped out soon.

The moon was bright enough so I could see the bomb shelter from my room. Cans of Spam were still stockpiled along the edge of the trench, and jars of water glowed in a neat line. The shovel stood up in a mound of dirt.

I crawled out my window and began taking down the trip wires I'd set up for Coyne. I sat at the edge of the pit, sprinkling dirt into the pool. A little later I went down in the bomb shelter again and waded through the water. Submerged cans of Spam hurt my feet as I stepped over them.

In the Mojave once on a full-moon night like this I had walked along the railroad tracks. The sand and rocks looked peculiar like a sight on the moon. A train with loads of borax was coming, and I lay down on my stomach only feet from the tracks to feel the roar. Moonlight made the borax in the open cars look incandescent, the soap Reagan would be peddling in ten years on TV.

On that Mojave night I saw a hobo climb up into the seat of a bulldozer freighted on a flatcar. The man held his hands on the steering wheel, pretending to drive. Then in slow motion, he waved to his left and to his right at no one in particular as if he were on a parade float doing something more important than being pulled through the desert on a train.

1952. The muddy water in the bomb shelter ringed my legs and rose higher. Something shifted in the top of a palm, went quiet, then swept over.

Maybe a Wave

On the rock, heat was constant, salt in the air thick enough to cure ham, and fear and booze the undercurrent. Nine hundred people living on a crust of coral in a nuclear proving ground and path of typhoons.

There were stories. Some sailor ran buck naked through the commissary. A captain deliberately swam into shark-infested waters. Our next-door neighbor wore nothing but a fur coat and doused her sleeping husband with a skillet of hot fat one night. He slipped her a tranquilizer and boarded her, limp in her greasy chinchilla, on the next plane to Honolulu. Island fever. It's what everyone called it.

A day before a typhoon alert on Kwaj in 1953 my mother got the chaplain to come to the house to talk to my father about his drinking. The chaplain was balding, wore black frame glasses, and had a gold cross pinned on the collar of his khaki short-sleeve shirt. He waited in the living room.

I was surprised my mother invited him. She grew up

with a Bible-thumping father and swore she'd never listen
to another sermon again.

"What's he here for?" my brother asked, looking
through college catalogs on his bed. Bubba was already making plans to get off the island as soon as he could. I was
still taking the high school correspondence course, but he'd
finished it early and was on a search for a college with the
ultimate bohemian atmosphere.

"Ask Mother why he's here," I said. "You can probably
guess."

"Christ," he said. But he was ashamed of our father's
drinking, too. Whenever things were going well and we were
settling into a new place, Jack seemed to sabotage it by drinking more.

When Jack got home, Matty grabbed him so he wouldn't
get away, yelled for the chaplain to come quick, and shut
them both in the kitchen. She guarded the door. It was over
in minutes. I watched from my room.

"Well?" Matty turned to the chaplain.

He and Jack both had drinks in their hands. "Well what?"
Jack rattled ice cubes in his drained glass as if they were dice
he intended to cast. He didn't take his eyes off her as he
sipped the last bit of his bourbon and crunched the ice.

"Matty," the chaplain said, "Jack and I have discussed
this. He's told me his side—the pressures he lives with at
home and with his job. Maybe if you just let up a little. You
can't force these things, you know."

My mother crossed her arms. "I can't believe it."

"Take it easy," my father snapped.

"You're all alike," she said. Her red hair was held back
with combs, and one was falling out. "The whole goddamned
bunch of you."

"Matty, please," the chaplain said, and touched her arm. "I know about these things."

"Go to hell," Matty said, nudging his arm away and pushing past them. She went in the kitchen, and we heard pots and pans banging. I knew dinner would be burnt.

My father went to the officers' club for the rest of the night. No one spoke at dinner, and Bubba started to read. The book cover had a picture of a gauzy amoeba membrane stretched over turquoise rings of Saturn.

"Put the book away," Matty said. "Some families talk, you know." She got up and wrapped wax paper over the extra pork chop for my father. "What are we going to do about getting you a nice wool sport coat?"

The Navy exchange didn't carry any here in the tropics. It was almost a year before Bubba would leave for college, but Matty was on it.

"God, not this again," Bubba said. "I don't want one. Nobody at Reed wears them."

Bubba told me students went barefoot to class and some were Communists. "There are things out there you're not going to have a clue about," he'd said to me. "Not a clue."

"Dammit, you need a nice sport coat," Matty yelled. "People will think you're a slob. You won't have friends."

"I give up," Bubba said, pushing back his chair.

Matty started clearing plates and running dishwater.

"Why'd you drag the minister here?" Bubba asked.

"I didn't drag anyone," she said, scrubbing a glass hard. "Obviously it was a mistake. The man's no different than your father."

"Why don't you just ignore what he does?" Bubba said.

"Ignore it? Don't get me started." She scowled at him over her shoulder. Bubba always said she looked like a pissed-off Rita Hayworth. Now lines were beginning to set in her face and she appeared angry, even when she wasn't.

"I live here," Bubba said. "I hear it. If I had to listen to someone nag me . . . I'd drink, too."

The water was running. My mother turned with a soapy spatula in her hand, her jaw set as if her whole being were focused on that moment. She walked forward and grabbed the edge of the table, still holding the spatula. Her grip made a small tear in the red plastic tablecloth. Water dripped off her elbow. "Don't let me ever hear you say that again."

I looked out the window. It was dark, but light from the kitchen threw a patch on the purple coleus outside.

Matty loosened her hold on the table and stood up.

"That man does what he wants and to hell with everyone else. It's always been that way. He's selfish. I could tell you some things." She pushed her hair away from her face. Her red hair had stopped my father cold almost twenty years before.

"What things?" Bubba asked.

"Never mind," she said.

"I want to know," he said.

"You think he's reliable?" Matty had a light sweat above her lip. She walked over to the window by the sink, looked out, and flicked the switch for the porch light. I'd seen my father dancing with a WAVE in Com-Closed once. The juke-box was playing "Cocktails for Two," and he stepped back when I walked in.

"An alcoholic makes everyone's life a living hell. And they don't change. I'm sick and tired of it." She blotted her forehead with a paper napkin.

I thought of my father as a casualty of history. He'd

joined the military during the Depression to have a steady job and got stuck in it. Jack was intelligent, but now the drinking was beginning to tell on him. He could be two different and complicated people, one charming, one cruel.

"What were you going to tell us?" Bubba asked.

"Some things you can't walk away from," Matty said.

"What are you getting at?" he said.

She bent down and leaned in closer to him. "Skipping out. That's what I'm getting at." She said it suddenly and looked startled. She stepped back from the table.

Bubba sat still, his eyes on her. Mother went to a drawer for Scotch tape and fiddled with the tablecloth. Her hands were shaking.

"Are you going to tell us?" Bubba said.

She set the tape down and went to the other window again. "It was a long time ago, before the war. Before we met. So let's just forget it."

"You can't leave it like that," Bubba said.

She smoothed her damp, wrinkled dress, distracted.

"We're going to imagine the worst if we don't know," I said.

She turned around and folded her arms, shaking her head. "He got some girl pregnant. I found old letters." She paused. "She wanted him to marry her, but he wouldn't have anything to do with her. She was Japanese. Never saw his daughter."

"Did you ask him?" I said.

"You don't ask about things like that," she said. "I put the letters away and didn't say a word. It was years ago." She fanned her neck, looking down at the linoleum. "Even if I asked, I wouldn't get the truth."

Bubba stood up. "I'm going to bed."

Mother walked over to the sink and folded her arms.

"Dammit, Bubba. I shouldn't have told you. But he makes me so damn mad sometimes."

Bubba flipped over the pages of his book.

"I'm sorry I said anything," she said.

"Yeah," he answered.

"God Almighty, I try. Don't turn me into the bad guy."

As early as I could remember, Japanese were the enemy. They were called Jap Rats, Japs, or Nips. During the war we lived in Seattle for a while, and life revolved around thwarting a Japanese invasion. We heard stories about how they still got through: an American family on a picnic in Oregon, blown up by a balloon bomb from Japan. I imagined the family finding it tangled in the branches of a spruce. Just a hot-air balloon from a circus.

We had siren alerts and hid under the kitchen table. Bubba and I laughed and tried to crawl out until Matty told us we could be blown up any minute by Japs. I always worried about that next minute.

We even lived in a house owned by Japanese who'd been sent to an internment camp. The bank took over the house and my father had a connection. We had never before lived off base. Never lived in a house with much of a yard. Naval housing was drab and crummy, with dried-up grass and kids' toys lying around. But this yard was clipped and neat with black pebble borders around cherry trees. There was even a goldfish pond.

The family had left a wire dress dummy in the garage, pressed into a tiny form, and a red cotton slipper in a puddle by the side of the house. On my closet door a girl had penciled her height and "Karen Hachiya 1940."

"You wouldn't have wanted to be in the Japs' shoes," my father said when we heard about Hiroshima. I imagined people screaming and thousands of shoes scattered. Karen Hachiya's shoe.

The night Matty told us about the Japanese woman, I went to Bubba's room to talk. "You don't know what happened," he said. "Maybe that woman made it up so he'd marry her, or maybe Mother read more into it than it was."

Once in a bar I heard my father talking about a sailor he knew in the war who fell in love with a girl. She told her family she was staying with friends, and she and the sailor set up housekeeping in a crate by the wharf when he was on leave. Made a bed of flattened cardboard, stayed drunk, and were happier than if they had a house of their own. But he was supposedly shipped out and killed during a bombing.

"A friend of yours, huh?" Matty had said at the time, glaring at him. Now I wondered if he'd really been telling his own story.

I tried to imagine the Japanese woman and the possibilities from one extreme to the other—someone who had meant nothing to him all the way to someone he'd loved.

"Wouldn't you feel something for your own child or sister?" I asked Bubba. "Maybe we've got a half sister out there. Aren't you interested?"

"There are things," he said as Matty had, "that are meant to be left alone."

Sometimes on Kwaj I imagined pine trees instead of palm and pandanus, ice instead of coral.

There was no spring on the island, and drinking water had to be extracted from the sea. At times it was even shipped in. A few weeks had passed since it had rained, so catchment water was brown and brackish, tingeing laundry.

"Damnest place in the world," my mother said, turning up the radio. "A desert in the middle of an ocean and half the time you're afraid of being washed away." News of an approaching storm broadcast from the radio.

A bad storm could mean a typhoon and tidal wave. Kwaj was only seven feet at the highest point, and when the alerts came, we had to go to the tallest place on the island, the chiefs' club. No one really knew if the two-story building could withstand a wall of water.

Bubba came in the house from a shortened scuba-diving trip with Jack. He grabbed a shirt and was headed out the door when Matty stopped him. "Bubba, last night. Forget I said anything. Erase. Erase." She made gestures as if she were erasing a chalkboard.

Bubba mumbled something like "I know," and looked out the window at Jack unloading the pickup.

Matty glanced out the window, waiting for Bubba to say something more. "Better go help your father," she said, and then went to the radio to tune in the fading weather report.

I went outside with Bubba to look at the shells. The backyard was strewn with finds from other dives. Clamshells, coral, and Chinese fishing floats—dark Coke bottle-green balls the size of globes.

Jack was trying to lift a giant clam, two feet across, from the back of the truck. He had a fishing knife on a belt slung over his blue swim trunks. His arms and shoulders were dark, and he was in good shape.

Bubba jumped in the bed of the truck, and they both strained, then pushed the clam off onto the sand. My father brought out a beer from the ice chest and took a long drink.

"How about a cold one?" he asked Bubba. He set a beer down for him and patted his arm. Bubba's freckled shoulders looked frail compared with my father's broad hand.

"He's going to be a tough nut to crack," Jack said. Bubba

teased at the red and blue fleshy mantle of the clam with his knife. My father wiped his forehead.

"Lucky will help with the shells. Won't you, honey?" He smiled.

Once when I hurt my arm, he held it under the faucet and turned it gently. He held my arm there for the longest time, lifting it up to the water. I was embarrassed; he'd never done anything like that. Maybe he was also thinking about his other daughter.

My father unloaded the ice chest from the truck and carried it inside. I started sorting through the net of shells, a red helmet, spider conchs, a map cowrie that looked like an ancient chart of islands and oceans in brown.

Bubba was still poking his knife at the opening of the clam. The scalloped valves were clamped tight. He slipped the knife into the mantle, up to his wrist. Then he slit through meat the length of the shell, severing the adductor muscle. That's when we heard voices from the house.

"I didn't mean it that way," Matty yelled.

"I bet you didn't," Jack snapped back.

Bubba pried open the halves of the clam. I scrubbed shells with a toothbrush in a bucket of bleach water.

"I should have known you'd tell them something like that," my father said.

"They already know what you're like."

When the yelling got bad, Bubba and I would take walks. He'd say, "Let's go see the horses," even if there weren't any.

Bubba was starting to cut out the white stringy muscle from the clam.

"You don't know anything about it," Jack yelled.

"I figured out enough," Matty said. "Leave me alone, dammit."

Bubba sliced off a piece of the ropy meat and offered it to me. I shook my head. "You told him," I said. "You told him what Mother said."

He took a bite of the meat, then wiped the knife handle on his trunks.

"I thought you didn't care," I said.

"We were just talking."

"So what's the story? He's got another kid someplace?"

He rolled his eyes. "He met some woman once and she made up a bunch of crazy stories later."

"That doesn't make sense."

"A lot doesn't. You hear it?" He pointed his knife toward the house. "Why do some people bother living like that?" Bubba stood up and tossed the meat in the sand. "Thank God I'll be moving out soon. I've waited for years. I'll be so goddamned glad to leave. You wouldn't believe." He threw the rest of the muscle in the bucket, then put his knife in its holder.

"It wouldn't be that easy for her to leave, you know," I said. "It's not like you going off to college. What would she do? Where would she go?"

Sand had whirled up in a dust devil. I tried to cover my eyes as I watched Bubba walk toward the house.

I came in when the sky darkened and the wind got too bad. In the kitchen I found Matty at the wringer washer furiously rubbing a bar of Fels Naptha over clothes that had turned a tea color from the water.

Wagner boomed oppressively from Bubba's phonograph. When we heard the alert, my father ran into his room and jerked the needle.

"Hey," Bubba yelled.

"Shut up. Listen," my father said.

I walked into Bubba's room, and we strained to hear. A warning to go to the chiefs' club sounded over the loudspeaker on the island bus. The voice repeated, fainter, as the bus moved on.

"Christ, what next?" Matty threw the bar of laundry soap in the kitchen sink and it cracked a plate and cups. She picked up the pieces of the dishes in both hands and paused as if she were trying to decide what to do; then she turned and smashed them into the sink.

By the time we left the house, gravel and sand were pocking the windows. Sand swept the island, making everything we passed in the truck look like an aged, grainy photograph. In the playground the swings climbed poles. One was flipping over the top bar. Waves on the seaward side of Kwaj crashed over the reef and onto the island. The road was wet from seawater.

We stood in line to go up the gray stairs to the club with our clothes and canteens of water. Behind us a little boy asked, "Are we going to die?"

I looked at my mother and thought of her breaking the dishes, but she stood quietly in place.

"At least the club is stocked with the best stuff," Jack said to Bubba. "They're going to show the motion picture early, too. *Bwana Devil.*"

Sometimes we went to movies at the chiefs' club. I'd seen *Bwana Devil* four times before, a 3-D color film we watched with special glasses. With the illusion of depth, things seemed to come off the screen: a locomotive in one movie. In another the audience gasped at spit propelling out of a cowboy's mouth.

We made our way up the stairs. In the club people were sitting in folding chairs and on the floor. The 3-D cardboard glasses were being passed out. Most of the red and green cellophane lenses were bent or missing. Without them the dual images on screen looked muddy and fractured.

My father went to the bar and stood with a group of his friends. My mother sat down on the floor, as if she were on the beach, and brought out a Marshallese fan from her purse to wave in the hot, sticky air. "You had to mention it to him," she said to Bubba.

Bubba started to say something, then: "You won't have to worry about me much longer."

"Lee," Matty said, "tell your father to get over here with his family."

"Bubba can do it," I said.

Bubba shook his head no.

"Lee, tell your father I want to talk to him," Matty said. Her voice was getting louder. People looked over in their colored glasses with the wrecked lenses. Matty pushed some loose strands of hair into her French twist. "For Godsake, we all might be dead soon," she snapped, and the goofy glasses turned away.

My father had his foot up on the rung of a chair. "I'll be there in a minute," he said when I walked toward him. He took a swallow from a long-necked beer bottle and tucked in his shirt.

I thought he should be with us like Matty said. "She wants to talk to you. She's sorry," I said, even though she hadn't said that.

My father turned to Teddy Barnes. "Aren't we all? Damned sorry we ever got lassoed in." Teddy laughed.

Jack pointed at me with the beer bottle. "But I'm not sorry the day you were born."

"Why don't you come back?" I said. Lights went off, and the movie was ready to start.

"I'll never forget that day she was born," my father said.

The projector started. Over the sound track Jack began telling his friends the story. A few other people made hissing sounds, and I felt humiliated. His voice rose louder as he went on about stealing a doctor's gown so he could get into the delivery room, climbing a tree to see through the hospital window.

I'd heard it before. "That's a lie," Matty had said when she overheard him once. "Don't tell her fool stories. You were passed out drunk. I walked to the hospital alone."

As we stood there in the club, I just felt embarrassed by him. But the first time I had heard the story, I had wanted my mother to stop and let us pretend how it wasn't. To let us change it to the way we would have wanted it. And now how the other daughter would have wanted it, not that blood would have made her anyone's daughter. Any more than it made her the enemy we hid from under the kitchen table.

I didn't know if it mattered anymore as we waited for a wave, for that next minute.

I glanced over at my mother across the room, waving her hand for us to come back. Whenever I started a new school, she would pin a small heart on my slip strap, the heart cut out from a scrap of cupboard liner, a paper napkin or bag, whatever was handy. On it she'd write, "I am brave. I am never afraid." I'd wear it for weeks.

But this time we wouldn't be afraid. No one believed we could die here. We would be out of this building in a few hours, laughing from relief, surprised by the island still there, talking about the part in the movie where man-eating lions are about to devour the natives. We were going to go about the business of being a family, as close right then as we could be to some lost brother or son, sister or daughter.

If a tidal wave had swamped the island and flushed

through the building, I know we would have looked for one another in that last 3-D rush of people and things.

But there was no tidal wave. Teddy Barnes took off his hat, put it on his dog, and gave him a pretzel. My father called for another round, and I went back to the movie. The images didn't merge, but I wouldn't look away from the spray of spears winging at us from the screen.

View from Kwaj

My father used the half skull of a Japanese gunner as an ashtray in his office and loved to tell how the Navy found the soldier in one of the bombed tunnels, holding a bottle of sake between his skeleton legs. "Hell, the booze was still good; we finished it off for him." He grinned as he leaned back in a rattan chair at Com-Closed with Teddy Barnes, Herschel Peck, and Max Knudson. They wore khaki shorts that flared a little like skirts, and their hats with gold eagles and spit-clean patent leather bills were always placed squarely in front of them, as if for inspection, while they drank from kelly green tumblers.

My father ordered Coca-Colas for my brother and me and a beer to loosen up my mother. We picked at greasy peanuts while the battles of the Pacific were recounted. It was 1954, but I didn't believe that World War II was really over.

In Com-Closed we had heard about an upcoming H-bomb test on Bikini, and from the start Bubba had wanted to photograph it for *Life* magazine. He usually took snapshots of exotic fish and shells from diving. He'd also gotten every teenage girl on the island to pose for him.

"All girls want to be photographed," Bubba told me. "You wouldn't believe what they'll do in front of a camera."

The snapshots of girls had been glued in my father's scrapbook of favorite bars. My mother had torn out the bar photos long ago, so all that was left were the names— Sharky's Horseshoe Lounge, the Acey Deucy—printed in white ink on the black paper. Now mixed in with the bar names were the girls' names in quotation marks beneath their pictures; "Carol" in a bathing suit, "Cookie" bending over in shorts, "Barb" stretched out on Bubba's bed in a prom dress, although there was no prom to go to on Kwaj.

Bubba got the idea to photograph the Bikini shot after Max Knudson started repeating rumors about it. "Anytime it could go off. The biggest, deadliest, motherfucking bomb ever. We might just see the pyrotechnics from our own back-yard." Max was dark with thick thighs, a chin that reminded me of the end of a potato, and a perpetually horny look on his face. I even spotted him eyeing my mother's legs once in Com-Closed.

"Figure a thousand times more juice than the one we dropped on the Japs," Max went on. "And the A got them whistling 'Dixie.' "

I waited for Herschel Peck to say something, but he didn't look up. He was rolling a swizzle stick around in his mouth and scratching Teddy's German shepherd, Wolfgang.

Herschel had been only miles from the first H-bomb blast. My father said Hersch could go to prison for discussing what he'd seen. But sometimes after a few drinks he'd talk. "We did our time in hell," Hersch said. "Like worms squirm-ing in a blaze when that fireball went up. I'll tell you one thing I'll never forget. After the blast. The damnedest thing. A little while after everything calmed down, we look out in the lagoon and the water's moving backward, like God parting the Red Sea. I swear it. We're seeing the ocean bottom, fish flopping around out of the water, an old B-25 that had been submerged. We just stood there in the freak show until we got hit by the shock wave and winds again. Knocked me flat on the beach. Then I look up at the lagoon. It's turned into this tidal wave about to pound us to shit. I'll admit it—I peed in my pants. I tore out of there faster than a striped-ass zebra. After that shot, mapmakers used a lot of pink erasers. We zeroed out an island playing God."

My father told us about the scientists on Eniwetok holding a fish up to some film and the thing photographing itself. When I asked Hersch, he wouldn't talk. "Get Bubba to figure it out," he said. "He's the genius."

Bubba said something about radiation.

"Hell, radiation," Hersch said. "What does anyone know? I'm healthy. That's all I care about."

From the beginning I was convinced that the bigger bombs meant another war coming that only we knew about. Or maybe everyone in the States knew something we didn't. We had no phones to the outside world, no TV, only limited radio, and newspapers and mail took over a week from Honolulu. "Face it," my mother said, "we're living in the outer reaches of the solar system."

Anything could be happening. But no one seemed worried. Maybe after not hearing from the outside world, everyone just lost interest. Service people were used to secret tests on remote bases. You didn't ask questions. Besides, the testing meant security. Max Knudson said it. "Up the ante on the bombs, and it's a surefire given: We'll never be the ones to get creamed."

★ ★ ★

"For Godsake, Lee, don't go running off with some sailor," my mother used to whisper to me in the kitchen.

"Where am I going to run?" I asked. Besides, I wouldn't have anything to do with sailors.

"Just make damn sure you know what you're getting into when you get married," she said. "Don't let anyone talk you into anything." It was a story I'd hear often. When she was eighteen, Matty had a job at Woolworth's, where my father bought candy bars. He flustered her at the cash register when he came in wearing his dark blue sailor uniform, tight across the rear, his hat pushed back at a cocky angle. Any man in a uniform was A-OK, and service life meant travel. She never dreamed of the places they'd stick bases.

"Pestered me until I said yes. All he really wanted was to sleep with me," she said. They were married in five months.

Besides my father, what continued to make her mad were the geckos—under the rugs, in shoes, the toaster. They'd even drop from the ceiling. My mother would swear and try to suck them up in her vacuum.

We all got tired of freezer-burned meat and canned vegetables. Nothing was ever fresh by the time it was shipped to us. Like the firs sent for Christmas—somebody's idea of a joke. They were a pile of brown needles when they arrived.

Unlike my father, who thought civilians and natives were inferior, I always felt there was something less about us. Something as second-rate as the olive green cans of surplus food we got in the commissary, the standard-issue sheets, the silverware stamped U.S. NAVY. I wanted to live in a tract house and stay put for years. Buy floral blankets and towels and get name-brand food with colored labels in grocery stores called Piggly Wiggly or A & P. Things on base were cheaper, but everything has its price.

I felt lonely, sorry for myself. I stood in front of the mirror wishing for somebody else's legs and chest and would work myself up for a cry.

I was also in love. Duke was Marshallese and exotic. He came from Ebeye every day with the other natives who worked on Kwaj. I fantasized about his fleshy lips, his faint mustache with light sweat. His name made me think of Duke Ellington or a title of royalty, even fists. Sometimes I called him the Duke.

He had tattoos done with a blue fountain pen: "Ebeye" spelled out, a letter on each finger of both hands.

Duke boxed groceries in the commissary, and I used to buy one thing so I could go through his line. He never looked up but flipped items from his left hand to his right, and when he got going, they became almost a blur. I'd always tip him thirty-five cents from my allowance. He didn't say much. I asked how he liked his job, and he only shrugged.

"Not one of those natives became a doctor, a lawyer, or anything," my mother said. "I hear they're still living in the Stone Age. Who could have ambition in this heat?"

We took the boat to Ebeye just to get off Kwaj and to buy things like shell jewelry and fans made of pandanus and feathers. Ebeye was the interisland trading post, and even offshore you could smell the rancid copra, the drying coconut the islanders traded. Skinny dogs and chickens ran loose, and empty bottles were piled on the beach. The natives lived in shacks and didn't use much furniture. "Lazy slopeheads," my father said. "You'd think they'd get sick of living like that."

I wanted to take Duke to the States, where he could go to school and get a good job. I wanted us to adopt him like the family who tried to bring their cleaning girl back with them. It was never allowed.

That didn't stop my plans. I imagined living on Ebeye, squatting in the sand and giving birth to light brown babies. Hormonal pull and suffering had everything to do with love, so I thought.

My father tried to tell Bubba there wouldn't be anything to photograph of Bikini. Jack had lost interest in filming the bomb blasts himself. His home movie camera no longer even worked.

"Hell, Max doesn't know what he's talking about, Bubble Eyes," my father said. "The bomb's a hundred seventy-five miles away, and you don't even know when it's going off. You'll be waiting around for nothing."

It didn't stop my brother. He got a new telephoto lens, bought every roll of Kodacolor film in the exchange, then set up a tripod on the beach and camped out, waiting for the blast. He tried to talk Carol, his old photo subject, into sleeping out, too, promising that she could be in some pictures. When she didn't go for it, I was second choice. "I guess you can camp out with me if you want," Bubba told me when he came home just long enough to pack sandwiches. His arms and face were sunburned, and his legs were dotted with mosquito bites.

"Max thinks it's about to blow," he said, biting into a cheese sandwich. "He's got a bet riding that they'll do it on the first."

March 1 was two days away. "How about if I brought someone?" I asked.

Bubba rolled his eyes. "Who? That hood from Ebeye?"

"Forget it," I said. "You don't know who I mean." But it was exactly who I meant. I'd been thinking about it for days. The problem was the Marshallese weren't supposed to spend the night on Kwajalein. "The Navy doesn't want any hanky-panky with the Ebeye natives," I'd heard my father say. But sailors would sometimes stay on Ebeye and walk the reef back after the last boat. I decided that Duke could do the same thing.

That night I lay on my bed looking at the ceiling, planning it. No one would recognize him easily on the beach at night, and in the morning he could hide out. I could even sneak him into my room.

I thought of us staying up all night together, and I had to do it. The next day I put on a pair of shorts and a T-shirt with a bleach spot so Duke wouldn't think this was any big deal for me, and I went to the commissary for his morning break.

Since he didn't know much English, I wasn't sure how I'd explain. He was behind the building, drinking an orange Nehi and smoking. "It's the Duke," I called out.

When I walked up, he smiled. I was as tall as he was, maybe taller. His white shirt was unbuttoned at the top, and his skin looked so smooth that it seemed poreless. He smelled like aftershave.

I knew he didn't have much time, so I jumped in about Bikini. I threw my arms out to show an explosion. "Maybe big fireworks tomorrow. The biggest ever. I'm going to stay on the beach all night."

He could see the same thing on his own island, but I had binoculars. I held my fists up to my eyes to show him. "You want to come? Stay on Kwajalein. It would be like a party. Like the Fourth of July." He looked confused. "Just come over on the reef like the sailors," I said, pointing to the water. "Hide out until you go to work." I nodded. "I even have beer. *Piyah.*" I knew a word or two in Marshallese, but nothing much. "Whatever you want. You name it."

Two box boys walked by smoking and spoke to Duke in Marshallese. He said something back, and they laughed.

"I don't know. It was just an idea." I shrugged. "It's only my brother and me. He won't be around much," I lied.

Oil glistened on Duke's hair. He ran his hand over loose strands. "Beach tomorrow?"

"Would it get you in trouble?"

"I do what I want," he said. Then he started toward his friends. "Hey, girl," he said, turning around. Right then when he looked at me, I thought he pursed his lips together like a kiss. I heard the other box boys laugh and make rooster-crowing sounds, but I didn't care. In less than twenty-four hours the Duke and I would be together. I couldn't stand it.

That night I cleaned my room, just in case Duke needed a place to hide. I put out the baskets and fans from Ebeye. After that I sliced up my legs shaving and then studied my work in the mirror.

The next day I went to the dock when the work crew was about to leave for Ebeye. I spotted Duke in the group playing mumblety-peg with some of the boys. That night was our secret, so I didn't say anything to him.

There were about fifty Marshallese on the dock, talking, some of them sitting on benches, tired from their day. Most of the men were in dungarees and T-shirts. Some of the women had on American-style dresses and carried purses.

Before they got on the boat, an MP checked them for stolen goods. With exaggeration, Duke held his hands high up over his head and turned around as the MP looked him over. He stalked away and gave a hand to Stella, the old woman who did ironing for a lieutenant's family. I watched as Duke leaned against the side of the boat and spit in the water. As they pulled out, I called his name, and he waved. "See you," I yelled, and pictured him walking back over the reef to be with me.

At home I packed beer and a bottle of whiskey in my knapsack and then headed to the beach. Bubba was fidgeting with the tripod when I found him. I spread out a blanket and started roasting hot dogs, leaving a few for Duke. Bubba and I weren't saying much. "A houseful of damn introverts," my mother would yell now and then. "Why doesn't someone talk?"

"For Christsake, you're smart enough," Bubba said suddenly when we were lying there watching the water. "Go to a good college like I'm doing and figure out what you want."

"What makes you think I'm so smart?" I should have known I wouldn't get more out of him.

"Put it this way. You don't seem as asinine as most girls your age." I was glad he didn't know.

Night was setting in, so I took a walk down the shore. A warm wind started up. I could taste the air and feel the grit under my nails. Sneaking drinks of a beer, I looked around for Duke.

I went back to Bubba and lay down as if I were going to sleep. With my eyes closed I pretended that Duke would be there when I opened them and I'd act surprised. I counted and knew each number took the possibility of him farther away. It was late now. He wasn't coming. I threw the extra hot dogs in the fire and watched them sizzle and blacken.

Duke probably knew from the beginning that he wouldn't come. I saw myself standing behind the commissary asking him to meet me, waving my arms around to describe the blast. Those box boys laughing.

"What's got you?" Bubba asked.

"How about a beer?" I said. We finished off the six-pack, and I kept looking for Duke in the shadows until Bubba asked why I was jerking around so much.

"Things never turn out the way you imagine them," I said. It was understood in our family. At Christmas after the presents my mother would say, "Is that it? Thank God it's over for another year," and the tree would come down by the end of the day.

A lot was like that. I'd pictured Duke's arm around me, his high school ring on a chain around my neck. But neither of us had a high school, and he hadn't even shown up. Reality never matched a fantasy. Maybe getting shots for *Life* was also just a fantasy, but I didn't say that to Bubba. He had even brought along two pair of welding goggles so we could observe the bomb flash.

The night was calm. The wind was dying down. I couldn't believe there would be a detonation. Hersch called it science fiction when the water shot up in the air and bloomed out with white orbits of electricity around it. During the flash the men had to sit facing the burst with their eyes closed. Then they were ordered to stand up and watch. Even with his eyes covered, Hersch had seen his own skeleton lit up through his skin, his bones X-rayed, like something out of *The War of the Worlds* when the earthlings were vaporized.

I thought about the men near Bikini sitting on top of an H-bomb that could be as annihilating as a Martian invasion, and I didn't blame them getting mindless drunk that night.

For years Bubba would describe the blast as the sun rising in the north that morning. He woke me up, screaming, "Jesus Christ Almighty!" We fumbled for the goggles.

The whole sky lit up a brilliant whitish yellow, brighter than day. A second later it changed to red, green, and yellow. Then the sky flamed in twisted shapes, and we saw the fireball blaze like a small sun for a moment just above the horizon.

Bubba was going crazy with the camera. "The cover of *Life,*" he yelled. "The cover! They'll eat it up."

In a few minutes the color was gone and it was dark again. Bubba put down his camera, and we took off the goggles, thinking the whole thing was over. Then the island shook. The sound came from below and above and pressed us down to the ground. Water in the lagoon slapped up in waves. I imagined the honeycomb of coral splintering and the island getting sucked below the water.

The vibration crawled up the buildings. Windows rattled, then popped and shattered. Garbage cans clattered over. Coconuts shook out of palm trees and whacked roofs. I huddled under the blanket and dug into the sand.

People were running out of their houses, as if it were an earthquake or fire. Bubba had a tight grip on the tripod and kept wiping his sweaty hands as he tried to hold the camera.

Finally the shaking stopped. We didn't move at first. The lagoon water was still sloshing. I looked back toward people on the beach in their bathrobes. As the sky got lighter, we could see a mass of clouds in the distance. The billows were spreading out. Bubba kept taking pictures and let me be in a few of the shots. We watched through binoculars as the clouds moved slowly eastward along the horizon.

I wondered if Duke was seeing this. Maybe he had been stopped coming to Kwaj. I decided I'd try to talk to him, learn his language. I wanted to tell him more about the H-bomb on Bikini.

Bubba was still shooting pictures when I started home with a headache from the beer.

I saw my father and Teddy Barnes, then a couple of WAVES come out of Com-Closed. One pretended to kick Teddy in the butt; then the two women walked off to the barracks, laughing. My father had spilled a drink on his shorts, and his usually slicked-back hair was rumpled. I noticed the wrinkles around his eyes and in his handsome tanned face.

"You missed it," I told them.

"Scared the piss out of Wolfgang and broke some bottles of damn good scotch," Teddy roared.

"I'll be a son of a bitch," my father said, looking at the sky. "Let's go see Bubble Eyes. I don't believe it. Bless his little old heart." As they walked off, Teddy was singing "Shake, Rattle, and Roll."

At our house the light bulbs had broken out of their sockets. My mother was sweeping them up along with some dishes. "I thought the damn walls would go next," she said.

The place was steaming. She'd closed the windows and had even pulled sheets off the line. My father opened the windows as soon as he got home. "For Christsake, the blast was miles away," he said. "We'll suffocate in here."

They argued about it, and the windows were opened, then closed, again and again the rest of the day.

Two days later a destroyer brought in eighty-two natives from Rongelap Atoll. "Dusted," Max told Bubba and me in whispers outside Com-Closed. "Fifteen megatons. Bravo shot. A hundred miles downwind from Bikini, and they get two inches of the fallout. Then winds dumped it over Utirik. We get those poor bastards in tomorrow."

Max looked off toward the wharf. "Christ, it was falling

on everyone. Now the islanders have bleeding burns and they're puking their guts out. We got the Marshallese out during other tests. What the hell's going on?"

The Rongelap islanders were checked over with Geiger counters that day and set up in the ship repair yard, separated from the people on Kwaj. Doctors were flown in from the States. "No significant danger," they would declare.

"What do you do?" Max Knudson said that day the ship with the islanders arrived. "There's no medicine you can give. We'll keep them off their islands for a while. Just have to wait and see what happens."

None of us knew that what would happen would be beyond what anyone could imagine.

The day after the Rongelap islanders were brought to Kwaj, I went to the dock to look for Duke. I was going to talk to him about the blast and find out what had happened to him that night. I took beer along in my Marshallese woven purse.

The ship from Utirik was in with 157 natives aboard, and they were still coming down the ramp when the work crew lined up for the ferry. The Ebeye people stared, pointing and talking as they watched the other islanders in the distance.

I wasn't sure how much Duke or any of the Ebeye people knew. There was no way anyone could explain what had occurred.

I finally saw Duke on the wharf. He and a boy in a faded blue shirt were sitting apart from the work crew. The boy saw me first and said, "Here comes that girl."

Duke was wearing a light orange shirt, the color of cream of tomato soup. His arms appeared hard and strong in the short sleeves. He looked better than I'd ever seen him.

I yelled out *iroij,* "chief" in Marshallese, and held up the beer. He whispered something to his friend as I headed over.

"You brought beer?" the friend said to me, stuffing gum in his mouth.

Duke got up and started throwing his knife into a wood barrel. I watched the quick jerk of his wrist, the black handle of the knife, and the blade flipping into wood with a whack. I waited for him to come over and explain why he hadn't shown up that night.

"What's wrong?" I finally said. "Why didn't you come to Kwaj? We watched the blast through binoculars. You could have really seen something."

Duke kept throwing the knife. Each time he went to get it, I thought he'd say something. The rest of the wharf—the sailors and natives and kids, the people coming off the ship— all of it disappeared. I waited.

Duke's friend said something to him in Marshallese and cracked his gum.

"Do you want a beer?" I asked Duke. I brought out the bottle and walked over close to him as he pulled the knife from the barrel. I could see the muscle in his arm tighten and the sweat on him. His skin would feel soft and damp. I tapped his shoulder gently with the beer. Right then, right as I wanted to touch him, he jerked away, his arm colliding with mine. I dropped the amber bottle, and it shattered on the dock. People looked over at us.

He bent over then and spit into the beer and broken glass. He looked up at me, moving juices around in his mouth, and spit again in the mess of foam and glass on the dock. He spit as if he could rid himself of all the spit inside. "Navy girl," he said. Only those words.

All I could do was hate him: the sweat on his upper lip, the blackness of his hair, his eyes that turned me into nothing but spit.

Even though I always swore I'd never sound like my father, I said it then. "You wouldn't have anything, not a thing, without us. You'd still be living in the Stone Age. Stupid slopehead."

Duke tightened the grip on his knife. His eyes fixed on me as if to aim. Then his eyes sent me out of my clothes, shoes, anything mine. Down to the tunnels where I was nothing, absolutely nothing. His eyes held me there until his friend laughed. Then Duke turned abruptly and walked away, as if suddenly I wasn't worth even his spit anymore.

Later I went over and over that scene. I saw his eyes and prickled with sweat, felt it down my back. For two days I didn't come out of my room. I stayed away from the commissary for a while, and I only saw him again from a distance.

In three years the Rongelap natives were returned to their island. They called that year, 1957, "the year of the animal." Some of the babies weren't human out there after we set the world on fire. Newborns took the form of jellyfish, bubbled blobs with hair, skinless creatures of some other world's design.

In my brother's photographs the clouds from Bravo look far away, some of them just like smudges above the water. The colors of the sky are so brilliant it's as if they aren't showing up true. The pictures never made it into *Life* magazine, but Bubba wrote neatly on each one "BIKINI H-BOMB, VIEW FROM KWAJ" and arranged them sequentially in a new album.

Included is a picture of me that my brother took in front of a hut on Ebeye. I'm wearing a straw hat to cover a frizzy home perm, and I have on a black bathing suit that looks as if it's made of vulcanized rubber and has what my mother called "bones" in the top. I've got a hibiscus in my hair, and I'm posing like Veronica Lake. In the background are some natives, one girl in a white cotton dress.

It was years before I noticed the cast of that peculiar island light over us all. And that girl. Her hands on her hips, staring me down with everything she's worth.

Light at the Equator

After Bravo shot, the downwind islanders were led to the lagoon each morning on Kwaj to wash off radiation with soap. The Navy exchange had donated striped beach towels and after-swim cover-ups with hoods.

The natives came to the water carrying the colorful towels, the bars of soap. The terry-cloth cover-ups went unused. Still in their clothes, the islanders moved slowly across the beach and eased into the water as if they were bruised to the marrow. The women in one group, men in another, turning away from each other.

A girl about my age touched soap to her legs under her dress. One young boy rubbed soap on his neck while he held up shorts that were too large for him. A man pitched the soap, floated, then went under for a few seconds. He came up and leaned backward, dipping his hair so it slicked down.

I watched with binoculars from a distance, looking out from under a straw hat as if this were a beach resort.

*   *   *

The day before the natives had been evacuated to Kwajalein, Army and Air Force men on Rongerik monitoring station— 125 miles east of the H-bomb blast on Bikini—were flown in to Kwaj on an Air-Sea Rescue plane.

A few days later I was at the officers' club before the trough opened for the regulars. I'd been drinking ginger ale and talking to Junie, the petty officer who worked as a bartender on his days off. The "Woody Woodpecker" song was on the jukebox when Muzzy Peterson padded in, wearing a hospital bathrobe and bedroom slippers. Muzzy had been one of the crew at the Rongerik weather station. With him was his wife, Doris. Joe Beebe, the pilot I used to call the Lone Ranger, came in also, recently returned from Korea and working as a rescue pilot. I didn't know then what had brought Joe Beebe back.

Muzzy looked like hell, eyes red and lips swollen, his face thin, raw like a weasel's stripped of fur. He and Beebe walked as if they were already in the bag, Beebe with his limp from World War II.

Beebe spotted me right off. "Hey, kid," he said with a look that stayed on me for a while. I'd seen him around the base a few times since his return. He must have figured out that I was seventeen now. One day I'd dry salt and sweat off him with my hair in the sweltering afternoons, but that time hadn't come yet.

Muzzy looked possessed, heading for the bar as if he'd dragged his tongue across the Sahara. "Something'll go down silky," he said, easing onto a stool.

Junie brought out a bottle of twelve-year scotch and set out glasses. "You look lousy, pal."

Muzzy was shaking and grabbed the bar. Before he even

got the drink in his mouth, the glass tumbled and the scotch made dark splashes down his blue cotton bathrobe.

"Liquid gold you're spilling, my friend," Junie said.

Doris tried to steady Muzzy as she sat down at the bar, the skirt of her yellow sundress spreading out on the stool like a parachute. "Let's get back before they miss you," she said.

"Like hell," Muzzy mumbled. "Give a guy last call before the next stinking hospital. No telling what tests they'll run at Tripler." The legs of his sky blue pajamas with dark piping were flappy around his white ankles. He pushed the sleeves of his robe up and clawed at his arms. Doris loosened the belt around his waist.

"So, shipping out to Honolulu," Junie said.

Muzzy undid a button on his pajamas and scratched at his red chest. Doris jerked his hand away. "My God, stop it," she ordered him, and stood up at the bar. She poured herself a drink and lit a cigarette from a gold pouch, then exhaled quickly—mad, fed up, or in despair, I couldn't tell.

Muzzy glanced at me as if he'd just noticed I was there. He motioned his head toward me, questioning Beebe whether I should be listening in to what he was about to say.

"I know Lee," Joe Beebe said. "No kid anymore." He winked at me. "Bar talk doesn't walk. She knows that."

Before I nodded, Muzzy had started in to Junie even as Junie was stepping over to lock the club door, tiptoeing across the waxed green-tiled floor so he wouldn't miss a word.

"No warning from headquarters on Eniwetok. No countdown." Muzzy turned on the stool toward Junie. "This motherfucker roared." He pounded the Formica counter twice with a weak fist. "Flung me against a wall, my ears shot to hell. Windows blown out. We're bull's-eye in the

Bikini shit storm. Those bastards knew we'd get it. For Christsake, we tracked prevailing troughs for weeks."

"Ease back, baby," Doris told him, touching his shoulder gently with her red shiny nails.

"Rad levels off the scale," Muzzy went on. "Kept radioing the bums to get us the hell out. No planes, headquarters tells us. A tropical blizzard and we're sweating like pigs. Croak us and get it the hell over with, I told the assholes. Forty-eight hours later we're still bundled up, waiting for evac."

"Some royal screwup?" Junie said, wiping glasses. "Someone going to get their ass reamed?"

"You tell me anything that makes sense," Muzzy said.

Beebe poured more scotch into Muzzy's glass and started talking. "A Japanese boat got snowed. The *Lucky Dragon* ran short on luck. No one got a warning. Rongelap baby out playing patty-cake in fallout." Beebe cleared his eyes. "Radiation burns, bleeding. Ash in the drinking water. Some old guy with a bad heart powders his chest with it. Deaf woman packed her ears to hear Jesus calling."

"Ooga-Booga to all us other assholes." Muzzy started hacking on the scotch, and Beebe stood up, putting his hand lightly on Muzzy's back. Muzzy couldn't hold down the drink and coughed it up in a napkin. He looked up at Joe like a kid to his mother who he thought might have the answers. Beebe helped him off to the men's. Doris followed them.

Junie lit a cigarette and hitched up his pants. "Hell of a note." He came around and sat at the bar, poured himself some of the scotch. He'd seen it all at Com-Closed and knew to keep his own mouth shut about the testing.

A few regulars started pounding at the door and yelling. "Yeah, yeah," Junie shouted. "The nurse is in."

★ ★ ★

I imagined the snowstorm sweeping through Kwaj, palms bent, the swirling fronds tracing circles like a pencil compass. All of us in an unceasing prayer of sweat, waiting in blown-out buildings, crawling over window glass and buckled linoleum that paled in the equatorial light.

What did the men on Rongerik do for two days? Drink bottles of warm beer, open K rations. Muzzy in layers of clothes, drawing up his legs, a bandanna over his nose and mouth to filter out the coral dust and fallout. But the islanders in the middle of it, arms outstretched to usher in the last day of the world, mouths open to receive. Later they'd hold their tongues up to Geiger counters that would measure the rems they'd taken in this communion.

The islands were a prism of deception. "Seven thousand miles downwind was so contaminated that survival might have depended upon prompt evacuation," one Atomic Energy Commission report said. "Of course there were no persons in the area." I read the deceitful report years later.

After the blast the AEC released a cover-up press release that we saw in two-month-old newspapers from the States. "Individuals were unexpectedly exposed to some radioactivity. There were no burns. All were reported well."

The story became that winds had shifted. My father told us that the AEC would make use of the exposed islanders for a study about radiation in humans. It was my brother who first suggested the darker slant: deliberate exposure. "Maybe it was all planned ahead of time," he said at the dinner table one night. "They'd use the natives as guinea pigs."

Guinea pigs to study radiation's effects. No shifting winds. No accident. I hadn't heard anyone come out and say it.

"This isn't some Nancy Drew mystery, you know," my

father said. "It's way over our heads. They got experts with more years' experience than what you two combined have been alive."

I couldn't believe my old man would have blind faith. Every morning before dawn my father woke with the alcoholic's feeling of impending doom, a cold-sweat panic about life. He'd sit in his Skivvies on the edge of the davenport and would run his hand over his face and hair, growling. "Jesus Christ. God Almighty. Son of a bitch. Fuck, shit, piss." But when the time called for appropriate fear, he didn't seem to have any. I was never sure how to react either, here or anywhere else.

It was all too complicated, too overwhelming, and the forces too powerful: Ike, the Atomic Energy Commission, the military. Americans on Kwaj just slept the great sleep.

The Rongelap natives had been 100 miles from ground zero, and the Utirik islanders, 275 miles downwind. I watched them as if they could ever provide an answer, cordoned off, as remote to us as outerspace aliens. They were housed on Kwaj in huge Quonset huts—elephant huts, we called them—in the ship repair yard. In a few days, the Utirik natives would be moved to tents on Ebeye.

During the war we'd lived in Idaho on a base used as a German POW camp that had some similarities to Kwaj. When the German soldiers arrived by train, they were herded off to a compound and guards were posted. But later the Germans were put to work as gardeners and maintenance men. Some of them even started a swing band and played for the base. The woman next door was caught in bed with the Bavarian sax player.

My mother, however, was always afraid some kraut would go berserk and try to avenge the homeland, doing us in with a hoe before escaping. She moved a dresser up against the front door at night and kept a gun handy, some oversize relic from the Spanish-American War.

I imagined the Marshallese staging an uprising on the island, coming to smother us in the night with the beach attire.

Every day, when the islanders headed back to the Quonset huts from the lagoon, I followed from a distance. A few Marshallese stayed outside the huts, talking and smoking. I watched with the binoculars through a chain-link fence around the compound.

One islander who didn't swim in the lagoon usually sat outside the huts, smoking by himself. He wore a black cowboy hat. One time I thought he noticed me watching the swimmers. I put down the binoculars, embarrassed, and walked away.

The next day, when the islanders went to the lagoon to bathe, I brought my father's scuba-diving gear down to the shore: the tanks and hoses, face mask, my fins. It was an insult in the face of what had happened, but it was a way to get closer.

I'd only done a little diving in shallow water, but I made a big deal about fiddling with the regulator, dipping the tanks, checking for leaks. With the face mask in place, I stepped in the water, bubbling on the surface, and looked out from the small oval window across the line of water to the natives. The islanders were all around the lagoon. Near the shore some older girls in long dresses were washing their hair. One girl's waist-length hair spread out like a net behind her.

I dived under. Farther out were sponges, scarlet coral, fish with lips and eyes that someone would dream up for rubber masks. A spectrum of neon fish schooled below me and swam through corroding war wreckage: a landing craft, plane propellors, deck guns. Over the wash of my own breaths through the hoses, I listened for the sound of the natives rinsing and dunking. The water carried the muted noise of fish biting coral and, later, rain beginning to pelt the surface.

I rose up to just below the waterline where the buckshot raindrops hit. I surfaced and lifted my mask to look across the lagoon at the islanders heading into shore.

Maybe they had come down to their lagoon something like this the day of Bravo when sound flattened in the blanketing. The men wading in until they were waist deep, arms out wide. Girls holding out their dresses to catch the ash. An old woman with her mouth open, salting her gums for new teeth. Coral spun under waves and boiled up. Rain from the bleached sky pitted the chickens, the baby on the beach patting snow.

At dusk that evening I walked by the shipyard. Docked M boats rocked in a dim light. The smell of heavy machinery oil and fuel mixed with seaweed from the reef.

Some of the islanders were standing outside their barracks. Inside one of the Quonset huts women were singing, something in Marshallese, almost a wailing. I'd heard natives on Ebeye singing in a church once and walked in later when no one was there. Pinned around the altar were red and yellow paper flowers, hopeful colors, expectant of something that I was afraid would never arrive.

I'd gotten the idea to bring out my father's diving gear from his boat and bring it to the compound. I didn't know if anyone at the Quonset huts would even see me outside the fence or care about the equipment, but I gathered together the tanks, mask, and fins and went over.

The singing had stopped. A few of the islanders were

still outside. Kids were yelling in the huts, getting ready for bed.

Lights lit up the sides of the buildings. I stepped closer to the fence, and a small cluster of natives noticed me. I knew how it looked, as if they were another species I was observing.

In the front of the building an MP was filling out something on a clipboard. Bobby Wiggins. He came over to the fence. "What's going on?" he said. A young guy with pimples that looked like tomato seeds on his face.

"Taking gear to the boat."

He turned around and glanced at the huts, then back at me. I stood there with the equipment, feeling foolish. I didn't know whether to get going or stay. He didn't say anything more but looked down at his clipboard and headed toward another MP.

Two girls had been watching me by the fence and came closer. Both in long dresses. One about fifteen wore her hair back in a scarf. The other was younger with a broad face and dimples, a red-print dress. Her hair was in a barrette. I noticed their arms right away, irritated and raw like Muzzy's, long streaks as if they'd clawed at them.

The pile of equipment by my feet got their attention. With a flashlight I shone a beam on the gear so they could see it better. I held up the black face mask to show them, then slipped the mask under the fence to the older girl. She put it up to her face and looked through the faceplate, turning her head from side to side, squeezing the rubber skirt.

I set down the blue rubber fins and nudged them under the fence, flashing a light. The younger girl slipped her feet into them. The other one knelt and bent up the ends of the blades. The girls were talking, rubbing their arms as they spoke.

I didn't notice the man with the cowboy hat when he first came over. His eyes were almost hidden under the brim of the hat. It took a moment for me to see when he got closer—his neck, arms, in the crooks of his arms, on his ears: large, upraised blackened areas.

The man had on khaki military-issue pants, a white T-shirt. Around a belt loop he'd wrapped a chain with a copper-colored St. Christopher medallion he'd probably picked up from a GI. He couldn't have worn the chain with the burns on his neck.

The man folded his arms so I wouldn't keep staring at them. The lesions made me think of splotches of black lacquer, chipping around the edges. Dark burns marked the tops of his feet. I tried not to look at the man. I wanted to get away.

I showed the girls how to breathe with the tanks, squatting down to inhale into the mouthpiece. The one with the scarf reached through the fence to touch the hoses. I held out the mouthpiece, and the girls made rubbery echoes into the hoses. I hoisted the tanks on my back, tugged the straps, and turned around. They poked their fingers through to feel everything, the straps, the tanks. One girl made a ringing sound by tapping her fingernail against a tank.

I turned around again. The man reached his fingers through the fence to touch a hose. Some of his fingernails were missing, the fingertips nude, blunt. His other nails were discolored, bluish brown. Without thinking, I pulled the hoses away. I had the impulse to keep everything from being touched by his sick, burned skin, as if he were a leper and could pass it on to me, the contamination, bad fortune. I was ashamed for thinking it, then and now. He put his hands in his pockets.

I was sweating in the sticky air with the smell of the shipyard. I took off the tanks. From the dock we could hear a mother on Kwaj yelling at her kids to get in the house.

The man put his feet down on the fins, flattening the openings and straps. He held the diving mask up to his face. I flipped the flashlight on to distract myself from him, and the beam accidentally glanced off the glass in the mask to his dark eyes and long lashes. He flinched.

Noise in the compound was winding down. But on the patio at the Pacific Club people were dancing to "Sentimental Journey." The older girl laughed and waved her hand to the music. We stood there on the dock, listening.

I thought of a ballroom that fell off the Santa Monica pier in the twenties with people still dancing inside. Maybe the lights had shone through the windows under the waves and the mirrored globe on the ceiling had kept rotating.

The two girls pointed to one of the huts and turned to leave. The man and I were left there as if we were at a dance waiting for the music to start. I looked toward the airstrip. Ground lights lit up two Air-Sea Rescue planes by the hangar, salvation too late for any downwinders.

I shone the flashlight into the dark, oily water, what was out there beyond us and the small spike of my flashlight, the depths of pitch, maybe hiding a shark. My bare legs were pale in the flashlight beam. The light shone through the fabric of my skirt.

I was deciding what to do. If we could loosen things up, I thought, we could do more than sleepwalk through this, mute as sticks. Even though he didn't know the words, I began to tell the man about snow, snow in Idaho, the prisoner of war camp.

The base became a ghost town after the war. I'd seen it

from a train once, I told him. The demolished clapboard housing, snow-powdered davenports, swirls of abandoned bedsprings.

I'd seen elk walking through our living room, eating grass shoots coming up through the bricks of the fireplace. An elk was lapping snow off the windshield of a rusted-out Hudson Hornet. To be inside the Hudson and see that tongue pressed up against the windshield, I laughed.

The islander was picking at the fence wire, no idea what I was saying, embarrassed at my voice getting too loud. I was talking more to myself. He looked around as if he were about to leave.

A gecko was somewhere close by, and I counted the number of sounds it made. Even—good luck. Odd—bad. Or it might have been the other way around.

I pointed toward the St. Christopher to ask where he'd gotten it, to keep him there longer. He undid the clasp and hung the chain on the fence.

I bent over to the scuba tanks. I wanted to prove something to myself, to make up for pulling away from him earlier. I pointed to the mouthpiece. I put the mouthpiece up to the fence so he could touch his mouth to it through the wire.

The cowboy hat was in his way. He pushed it back on his head. When he did, some of his hair fell in his eyes. He felt the hair, lifted the black strands. They kept lifting, coming forward in his hand. He dropped the hair.

The man raised the hat up, then higher, revealing a geography of bare patches on his head. He felt his scalp, palming it. Strands fell out easily. I tried to reach in to smooth his hair, coarse silk thread. The tight weave of the fence prevented it. I bumped the chain of sour metal beads hanging on the fence, and then brushed against his arm and some hair that had stuck to his damp skin.

Moths kept bumping the screens on the Quonset huts to get in, tropical moths that looked like rodents on wings. The band at the club was playing "Sing, Sing, Sing."

From inside the nearby hut sounds were coming from one of the islanders. The man and I looked over, trying to make it out. Someone talking from a faraway sleep.

In Idaho, it was almost dusk, deep blue, when my father would walk the path back from the icy creek, carrying a fly rod, a cluster of fresh rainbow in his hand. There was a chill in the late afternoon, the sound of the stream over rocks. Miles and years away now.

I began gathering up the nest of hair into the cowboy hat.

Swear

In the spring of 1954 my brother looked away from Kwaj, as far as he could. He built a telescope in the backyard, a Newtonian reflector, he called it, over five feet long and able to shoot pictures of the moon and star clusters.

Bubba would stay up most of the night watching the sky and developing pictures in the bathroom, or he'd lie in bed reading, taking Bromos for a jumpy stomach, all the while not talking much to anyone.

Then he disappeared. He was missing all night. In the morning I searched the WW II Japanese tunnels we'd explored. A few months before, we had discovered the remains of a soldier in one. That's where I found Bubba.

For a day he was in a coma, poisoned from too much alcohol. As my mother and I walked home from the hospital, I think she suddenly saw this as only the beginning. At the steps of our house, she got dizzy and held on to a hibiscus bush, a red blossom wadding in her hand like a tissue.

★   ★   ★

As soon as my brother was back from the hospital, Matty brought him a BLT and a milk shake, still in the Waring blender, and tried to get him to talk about what happened. My father was on a detail at another base for a week.

I was outside Bubba's door and couldn't see him but knew he was lying on his bed pretending that Matty wasn't there trying to talk to him. She kept asking him why he had pulled such a crazy stunt. Her voice was shaky. "Tell me what's wrong. The doctor said you must have guzzled that liquor like you were bent on never coming out."

"Forget it. Leave me alone."

"God Almighty, you almost died." Her voice rose. "Put that book down." I heard a hand slap a cover and the book tumble and thump the floor. "Don't you think I care?"

My brother said something in a low voice that I thought was going to tell us everything. I'd been waiting for him to say it was a mistake, a goofy teenage caper we'd discount in a few years. It took me a second to figure out what he'd said to her. "There's nothing to talk about. Close the door on the way out."

"I'm your mother. Now talk to me, dammit." That did it. He'd never say a word for days now. There was a long silence, and then her voice cut through the cheap walls of naval housing. "What the hell's the use?" She rushed out of the room, taking the BLT and milk shake back to the kitchen.

When I looked through the door, Bubba's bare back was to me, thin as if someone had pulled and formed it in clay. Suddenly he turned as though he sensed I was watching him. He got up. His khaki shorts were baggy around his waist from the weight he'd lost, and he pulled them up as he concentrated on something behind me. Then he shut the door.

More than he'd ever been, Bubba was beyond me. It

was as if he were at the bottom of some deep pool, and the things he understood were fathoms from my reach. But sometimes I imagined what it would be like if his brilliance and remoteness were suddenly removed—like in a car accident—gone in the spider web of windshield glass so I could finally understand him.

I stood and listened at his door that day, but there was nothing to hear.

My mother was missing the next day. She was gone through lunch, then dinner. I walked by the kitchen as Bubba fried up a bacon and egg sandwich for dinner. When he headed out toward the beach with the sandwich, I thought he wouldn't notice me following.

"See you later," he yelled, not even turning around. I hung back but tracked him for a while as he walked by an old ship anchor in the playground and started around the island.

My mother was sitting in the living room with the lights off when I got back. She turned on a lamp and covered her eyes with her hand. I sat down in one of the rattan chairs.

"I keep trying to figure out what I did to him. I should know," she said. "I had no business having kids. I was too damn ignorant."

She pulled out a thread on a cushion and examined the davenport for more loose stitches. "Those days you meet someone. Think you like them well enough. Get married. Have a baby. Maybe you don't even want it. Fourteen kids in my family. I don't remember my mother even touching me." She rubbed her forehead. "You can't give more than the nothing you've got, Lee. I didn't have anything to give kids. I didn't know how." She looked at me as if searching for an answer she already knew didn't exist.

"You did your best," I told her. "You couldn't do anything more than that."

"Being ignorant's no excuse. Ignorance of gravity doesn't stop a dish from falling and breaking. Someone's to blame, someone's to account."

"You can't blame yourself for this."

"But I'm his mother."

"You're too hard on yourself," I told her. "Bubba's okay."

"The doctor thought it was serious."

"It was an accident. He just got drunk and didn't know what he was doing." I wanted to believe it. I looked at her to see if she did.

She reached over and touched my hand. "Thank God you're here. What would I do without you?"

"Don't say that."

"Why shouldn't I say that? It's different with a daughter. With a girl. I can talk to you."

But a week before, we'd gotten into an argument and I'd run out of the house, slamming the front door. I'd yanked so hard on the doorknob that screws had started to twist out of the wood. "You just watch it, sister," she'd yelled after me. "You're not out of this house yet." But I was. I was seventeen and gone in ways she refused to see.

"I couldn't talk to Jim," she said. She called him by his real name sometimes instead of my father's nickname for him. "Then he became so smart I was afraid of him. Now it's hopeless."

"How can you say that?"

"He won't let me help him. He doesn't want anything to do with us."

It was true my brother had tuned her out a long time

ago. Matty saw life through her austere past and fired out stern, outdated advice in a back hills way of talking. And Jack just didn't know what to say to us.

"I got some books out of the library," Matty said. The library was a few shelves in an old barracks with mostly *Reader's Digest Condensed Books* and back issues of *Stars and Stripes*.

Mother pulled some books out from under the couch— one about living through those teen years and Dr. Spock's *Common Sense Book of Baby and Child Care.* "I want to see where I fouled up, from the beginning all the way through," she said. "This other one might be good for Bubba." She held up *The Art of Real Happiness.* I didn't want to tell her that he wouldn't even crack that open. He'd howl at the title.

She put down the books and looked at me as if she had something else to say but didn't know how to start. "I went to a seer today, this native lady on Ebeye I heard about. They say she knows things, Lee, before they happen. Conjures the future. She's saved lives that way."

"You believe that?" I said. My mother had told me about the seer in the Ozarks who could supposedly locate a lost cow or jewelry. But I didn't think my mother believed anything except that life was a struggle and full of hard work. She called people who went to church sheep and ranted about the Marshallese being bamboozled by Christianity. One time in the States I told her a story I'd heard in a church service: a family trapped in their car on railroad tracks and the engine starting when the father yelled, "Jesus, give us salvation!"

"All churches have that damned old car-on-the-railroad-track story," Matty had said when I told her. "People will believe anything."

"What did the seer say about Bubba?" I asked her now.

"She didn't say much. Told me I can't chase after him. Whatever that means. After that she stopped."

"You ask her anything more?" I said.

"She's probably a crackpot. She talked funny. Had a voice like a kid when she went in her trance. You should have seen the place. Swarming with flies. Dirty. No water or electricity. Not a stick of furniture."

"She went in a trance?" I asked.

"She was taking breaths funny."

"What else did she say? Tell me everything."

"I told you," my mother said. "Don't hound me. It was silly to go there."

I stayed up that night and thought about the seer, why she'd hushed up and what it was she saw. Certainties we'd want to believe. Or ones we'd fear and refuse to accept, even after they had happened. What I had wanted was only a promise that everything would be okay. But I would never be able to hear that.

The next morning, while Bubba was outside, I went to his room and checked for clues about what he was up to. I looked through his science books and at a chalkboard with equations all over it. I tried to imagine what any of the marks on the board meant, as if they could tell me how to decipher him.

He had up pictures he'd taken with the telescope: moon phases, stars that looked like pinpricks against gray or just bad film with white spots. He'd filed his negatives in envelopes labeled with names like Andromeda and Cassiopeia.

I picked up some punched-out circles from notebook paper he'd filed in his astronomy log, and I stuck a bunch in my pocket. Then I went to the window and looked out at the yard where Bubba was. He had his back to me and was fiddling with the telescope. I never understood how he constructed it. He'd used materials on Kwaj and parts he'd sent away for.

As I watched him, I was thinking about his riding me on his friend's motorcycle when we lived in the Mojave. When I held on, I tried to breathe like Bubba, inhale and exhale at the same time, as if that could make me think like him or bring him closer. Sometimes I got off the motorcycle imagining my IQ had gone up a few points.

As I stood at the window, I was thinking about the tunnel. I wanted to understand his trip from the galaxy down into the island. I had to go there.

Most of the trenches and tunnels had been filled in since the war. The entrance to the one we went to was hidden under bushes and vines. I crouched down and slid in through a tangle of leaves, gagging on coral dust that sprayed up. Inside, the air was almost too heavy to breathe, so salty I could taste it.

Rifle cartridges, coral, and broken seashells pressed into my knees and hands as I crawled in. Bubba's empty bottles were scattered around the tunnel. I lined them up in a row and put one to my mouth. There was a woody aftertaste.

I wanted to understand what brought Bubba and me together, separated us. I thought one thing was that I was too emotional and cried easily. "Jesus Christ, there she goes again," he'd say. Emotion showed stupidity; depression was a sign of genius.

My mother tried to find reasons for Bubba's depression. It was from moving around so much, being uprooted. She even thought it might be world events that made him moody: the Cold War, blacklisting, attacks on Oppenheimer. She repeated an Adlai Stevenson line like a comforting saying: "The way of the egghead is hard."

Bubba was the hope of the family. It was as if his intellect would lift the whole family up from white trash status. A mind for science was what the country needed in the Cold War.

I moved farther into the tunnel. The day Bubba and I found the soldier's remains, I screamed and Bubba grabbed the flashlight, then crawled in closer. I stayed back but followed the light over the threads of a sleeve. The skeletal legs were bent and leaned against the wall. The rib cage was thrust upward and tilted at a funny angle. Buttons from the uniform had dropped through to the backbone.

Fascinated, Bubba had moved even nearer to study it. Alongside the spine lay the top half of a photo, a young Japanese woman carrying her baby in a sling on her back, something the soldier looked at and held to when troops took the island and flamethrowers flushed out tunnels. The soldier must have memorized each detail of his hideout: the salty dust, how he sweat into his clothes. He craved the taste of an orange, to hear music again, to stay alive for his family.

I laid my head down on the damp ground. This must be what it's like to give up. The skull finally dull with mud— no more desire, emotion, equations.

When I got home, Bubba was on the ladder with his T-shirt off and was taking the telescope apart to clean a lens. His arms were as freckled as a leopard cowrie shell.

"Something wrong?" he said when he caught me staring at him. I shook my head. I went over by him and checked some chambered nautilus shells he'd buried in the sand so ants would clean out the meat inside. The pearly shells were busy with red ants and stank in the heat.

A prop plane went by overhead, and we both watched until it was out of sight. A year before, one went down with six nurses aboard. Sharks got everyone before a rescue boat could reach them.

"You remember Cindi?" I asked Bubba. She was one of the nurses. "Ever think about her?"

"I never really knew her."

A few weeks before the accident she danced with Bubba at the club when "Crazy Man Crazy" played on the jukebox. I watched the whole thing from the door. I never thought Bubba would get up and dance when she asked him. He jerked on the floor, his shirt too big on him. Cindi held a cigarette while she moved. She had pale skin and dark hair, pinned up in a bun, and wore coral lipstick. Her legs looked sturdy, powerful in white stockings, dancing, not knowing what would happen soon.

"You danced with her," I said. "Remember?"

Bubba didn't answer. Suddenly I said, "What if you'd died?"

He adjusted something on the telescope.

"What was it like being in the coma?" I tried.

"Colors," he said, as if he started to hear me. "Coming out of it, you see colors. Brilliant ones. I could hear what people were saying in the room, too, the whole time. You said you wanted to get the hell out."

"No, I didn't."

"Sure you did. I heard it." He laughed.

"I don't want you to die, Bubba."

"What's with you anyway?" he said.

"Do you want to die?"

He ignored me.

"Don't you care about yourself? About us?"

He concentrated on the telescope, and suddenly I became nonexistent.

I started rooting up all the shells. The ants were scattering. I grabbed a nautilus and pitched it along the ground so it skimmed the sand toward the telescope base. The shell clunked the metal. The curved end of the chambered nautilus chipped off.

"Christ. Would you grow up?" Bubba got down from the ladder. He began burying the shells again, the red ants crawling his red freckled hands.

Sunday my father came home. Bubba ducked behind the house as soon as he saw him pull up in the pickup.

Jack was in his khaki uniform and carried a suit bag and a briefcase. Matty went out to the truck and followed him into the house, filling him in on the details of what had happened.

I looked out the living-room window and saw Bubba by the side of the house, listening.

"It wasn't just a prank, Jack," Matty said as she closed the front door.

"Come on, he's just a kid," my father said.

"You try to talk to him. He cuts me off. Cuts me right off."

"Settle down. He'll come to me if he has something to say." He headed into the kitchen.

My mother stood in the middle of the living room with her hands on her hips. "That's it. Stick your head in the sand. I wouldn't expect anything more from you."

I knew when to get out and left.

Bubba wasn't anywhere in the yard. When my father drove in, he had been touching up the telescope with sealant. The can was still open, and the brush was drying in the heat, something Bubba would never do. I walked down to the beach, and when I didn't see him, I went home for a flashlight and then to the tunnel.

I called out to him at the entrance. When I crawled in, he had his Swiss Army knife out and was cleaning off the blades.

"Jack's home, huh?" he said. "Gangway for an officer."

"What are you doing?" I flashed my light on his knife and the row of empty bottles.

"Don't worry about it."

"Why don't you come home? I hate this place."

"I didn't ask you to follow me."

"What do you expect?" I snapped back.

His voice softened when he realized I was mad. "Remember the first time we were here? I've never seen anyone more desperate to get out of a place." He laughed. "It was right over there." He pointed farther back in the tunnel.

That day Bubba had run the light back and forth over the remains, and I'd hidden behind him, crying.

"Stop," he'd told me then. "Just stop. They're only bones, Lee. The guy doesn't feel a thing anymore. Home free. Nothing."

"Mother went to a seer about you." I said it even though I wasn't going to.

"A seer?" he said. "Like a fortune teller? Jesus. She really is going crazy."

"She's worried. So am I."

"Don't start."

"Was it just an accident?"

"I don't need that right now," he said, pulling each blade out.

I crawled closer, grazing my knees on the coral. "I want to know. Did you do it on purpose?" I waited for him to say something. Pressed against the wall, I scraped my back on pieces of shell embedded in the dirt.

"Would you promise me? Would you swear to me it'll

never happen again?" My voice sounded silly, awkward, and he caught it.

"You're talking like a kid." He snapped one of the knife blades into place, cutting his index finger against a smaller blade. "Dammit," he said, shaking his hand.

"I can't stand wondering what you'll do next. Going through it over and over."

"I thought you wanted to get out of here." He examined his cut finger, then wiped it against his blue jeans.

"Don't do this to me. Say something," I said.

He picked up an empty rifle cartridge in his other hand and rubbed it clean with his thumb.

"Goddammit. Look at me," I said. "Say something."

He looked up as if I had just spoken, then flicked his thumbnail over the top of the casing, whittling at it.

I raised my arm and put the back of my hand up to the sharp edge of a seashell in the ceiling. I jammed my hand up hard against the lip so it dug into the skin.

"What the hell you think you're doing?"

I worked against the shell edge, slicing deeper into my hand. During the invasion of Kwajalein, a tunneled-in Japanese infantryman short on weapons tried to slit his wrists with a seashell rather than surface to defeat.

I put my hand in front of Bubba and held the flashlight on the bloody cut. "Give me your finger," I ordered him, and grabbed for his hand. "You're going to swear to me you won't do anything again. Swear in blood. I'll believe it then."

"For Godsake, Lee." He threw the casing, and it chinked against the side of the tunnel. "Jesus, your drama. No one can promise anything like that."

I leaned over and punched him in the arm, then grabbed

the sleeve of his T-shirt, stretching it out, swiping it with blood. "What about me? Isn't that enough? Aren't I enough?"

"It doesn't have anything to do with you." Bubba pulled a handkerchief out of his pants pocket and handed it over without looking at me. "It's just the way it is."

"It's not the way it is," I screamed at him. I balled up the handkerchief and threw it down. "You can't. I won't let you, dammit. Nothing's that way."

He picked up the handkerchief and folded it into a triangle. "Hey, mad monkey face," he said. He rolled up two ends and pulled the other ends out. "Look at something dumb. A couple of people in a hammock. We're in the hammock swinging." He swung the stained cloth, then laughed.

That night I stood on the porch in the dark, watching Bubba sight through his telescope. He'd look for a while, then use the dim beam of his flashlight to check an astronomy chart.

Lights in all the houses were on, rows of them down the island. I could hear voices and radios from houses. The sound of the surf came suddenly. It was always there; we just forgot the constant pounding against the reef.

Later that night, when Bubba was asleep, I went into his room. His mouth was opened slightly, one arm over the sheet. Softly, without his knowing it, I touched the bloodied cut on my hand to the slash on his finger.

I got down on the floor alongside his bed. The rug was made of hemp and was scratchy. Geckos roamed the house, and I thought of one crawling over me, but I stayed anyway. "What a dopey thing to do," Bubba would say in the morning.

But that night I curled my legs into my nightgown and

waited. It was the beginning of waiting. Years from now he'd make his decision, breaking this unknown pact.

On that island, I knew what ran below us—under the playground; below the houses separated by the neat rows of clotheslines.

Angle of Incidence

In 1954 I watched my father dive off the overturned *Prinz Eugen,* a cruiser from the target fleet set up in Bikini lagoon eight years before. The two thirteen-kiloton atom bombs in Operation Crossroads had made a roaring brew of abandoned warships, some turning to mist, as they funneled up mile-high spouts.

My father and I were out in a boat, fishing with Doc Savage, a skipper, and Joe Beebe. It was early summer, and my brother had recently left for college in the States.

Doc, Beebe, and my father had all been drinking thick charcoal-tasting coffee laced with coconut hooch. Doc had brought the mascot monkey, Skeeter, along, and even he took a sip.

Joe Beebe sat across from me and kept pulling his Dodger cap low and winking. He called me babe and sugar when my father wasn't near. I made a face, but I liked it. No one ever called me anything like that. I thought I was too old for my nickname, Lucky.

My father got Doc to stop the boat when he saw the

Eugen. "Glory of the German fleet," Jack said, admiring it. I tried to imagine what the war cruiser had once been before the U.S. took it from the Germans and used it for target practice. "I've got to hand it to those krauts," he went on. "That was one goddamn beautiful ship."

I never saw ships in his way, as beautiful. Especially not a rusted soup can turned turtle with just the rudder and screws showing, the bridge and superstructure crumpled at the bottom.

Ships like the *Eugen* that hadn't sunk at Bikini were towed to Kwaj, scrubbed with lye and acid, and sandblasted to get the radiation out. The Geiger counters still went crazy. Finally the military gave up and scuttled the ships. Tugs had tried to beach the *Eugen* on Enubuj, a deserted islet, but she'd rolled over starboard and stuck on the reef.

We called her a ghost ship. The other vessels were submerged around the islands, ditched like rusty old cars run down banks or pushed into creek beds. Everything was on them when they went through the bombs: equipment, paper, dishes. I'd even heard wild stories of stallions on board jumping through shields of glass.

Usually we'd chuck beer or Coke bottles against the side of the *Eugen* and make a joke about christening her. Bottles made a dull clunk against the side of the hull, and then the glass would shatter like crystal.

"Nothing but a goddamn pile of scrap," Doc said, tapping ash from his pipe against the side of his boat. He had a huge stomach like a Buddha, the only part of him getting sunburned. Skeeter perched on his shoulder under the shade of a broad-brimmed straw hat.

"Geiger counter needles used to jump the scale near her," Beebe said. "She's hotter than a chili pepper."

"Eh." My father dismissed him with a jerk of his arm.

"Been years, ace." My old man was jealous that Beebe had been a reconnaissance pilot in the testing, was a lot younger, and had jumped him in rank. Jack was also frosty about Beebe's being in the Air Force, not the Navy.

"He's too damn slick," I'd overheard my old man say. "I'd trust that Joe Beebe about as far as I could kick him." He called him "that Joe Beebe" all the time to keep him at a distance. My father didn't know Doc had invited Joe Beebe that day, or we wouldn't have been there.

"Commanding officer out on Bikini used to strip down to his Skivvies after a shot and jump in the lagoon, ace," my father said to Beebe. "He's still walking around."

Joe Beebe shook his head and looked at me.

My father stood up and tossed off his khaki Navy cap. He hitched up his swim trunks and walked unevenly to the side of the boat, lipping a cigarette. Suddenly he dived over the side. He turned on his back to look at us, the butt of the cigarette still between his teeth. "So long, suckers," he shouted.

Doc didn't say anything. I wouldn't look at Joe. Maybe I was proud of my father as he headed to the *Eugen,* doing the backstroke as gracefully as a performer in the water follies, his arms cutting the water so there was no splash. We watched as he hoisted himself onto the rudder of the *Eugen,* and I understood the perfect sense of it. Of him on the blown-up glory of the German fleet. A displaced military man, mired in a rank and marooned on a sandpile in the Pacific—the sense of his standing on that ship. He was thirty-eight then, trim, wearing black swim trunks that came up high on his waist. My old man stretched his arms out so they made two ninety-degree angles with his body. He sprang a little as if he were on a diving board, and then he dived in precise form.

★ ★ ★

Diving off the *Eugen* that day set something off in my father. I found out what he'd started doing when things appeared suddenly on a shelf at home. There was the remnant of a phonograph record—wafer-thin, half dissolved, with crystallized salt covering it. A five-inch piece of handrail, lacy with rust, and a fork were also displayed on the shelf like golf trophies.

I walked into the kitchen where my father was telling my mother that he wanted his steak served on a plate he had in his hand—a white plate with the German black eagle on the rim.

"Get that contaminated thing out of here," my mother said. "I wouldn't touch it with a ten-foot pole." Matty was against the counter, her face gathered in a disturbed look. She wore a green striped sundress, and her hair was swept up in a ponytail.

"These things are priceless." He grinned.

"Keep away from that old tub. It's not safe," my mother said.

"A little hobby. A few souvenirs." Jack looked at me. "Lucky likes them." He motioned with his head for me to follow him to the living room. I watched as he set the plate upright on the shelf. "Did you see the record?" he asked. "Probably Strauss waltzes." He moved his hands as if he were conducting. "What do you think? Mount it on felt?" He adjusted the piece of record in various positions for display.

Maybe it was the danger of the dive or the possibility of getting caught that attracted Jack, the idea of doing what was forbidden, lifting and secreting the booty. All of it was just sitting there with only something invisible covering it, and if my father couldn't see something, it didn't exist.

I wouldn't understand for years that the testing made

him feel as if he belonged to something important, more than he ever had. It was larger than anything would be again in his life.

Like my father, I was sucked in, too. That night I took the melted phonograph record from the shelf and carried it with gloved hands to the record player. I wondered if the bomb had recorded itself over the waltzes. Out here ordinary things could twist into unnatural occurrences. I switched on the record player, listening for just a sound.

When my father was about to sneak off to dive into the *Eugen* the next day, I begged him to take me with him. I liked the idea of exploring a ghost ship, finding artifacts stopped in time, in mid-scene, at the instant of impact.

"Forget it," he said. He didn't trust me in the deep. The lungs could burst, and air bubbles in the blood could cause convulsions, brain damage, death. I'd also heard what the bends had done to pearl divers, leaving them crippled and bent. Only in water did they uncurl.

"You need a partner," I told my father. He ignored me as he inspected the nickel-colored tanks and the hoses. Then he put the mouthpiece in and tested it.

"What if I stayed on the boat?" I asked him. He shrugged and then nodded, but I got the impression that my presence there would be an intrusion for him.

We took the motorboat, a 16-foot Chris-Craft with an umbrella for shade. The boat was called the *Delores Ann,* but my father had been saying he was going to repaint it the *Lucky Lee.*

Jack wasn't saying much on the way out. He drank his coffee and operated the boat effortlessly. A few minutes later we put down close to the *Eugen.* Great flows of rust stained what we could see of the belly-up ship. Suddenly I was afraid for my father, imagining him lost in the maze of narrow corridors. Whatever desire I'd had to investigate the cruiser was gone.

My old man was rubbing tobacco from his cigarette into his face mask to defog it. Then he spit in it and sloshed water around. He hauled the tanks out and adjusted the flukes.

"Sure this is okay?" I asked him.

"Chickening out? You're not even diving."

I looked over at the *Eugen* again, imagining all sorts of tragedies in there.

"Just trust your old man," he said, and went about checking his gear.

"Are the Geigers gone?" I asked him.

"It's safe. What the hell's the problem after all these years? It's been soaking in brine. Ace just likes to think he knows everything."

"Maybe I could go snorkeling by the ship, Daddy." I always called him Daddy even though I thought I was too old for it. But the name "Dad" seemed too much like a pal.

"You just wait here," he said, and pointed to the boat seat. He put the mouthpiece in, testing the valve again, then slipped the tanks over his T-shirt, hitched up the harness, and put on the fins. He adjusted the mask and crisply saluted.

"Bombs over Tokyo," he said, as he did a backward roll off the side. I watched him swim over to the ship. The wreckage made me think of a mad fun house, everything hanging upside down—the bunks and commodes, the crew's table. I imagined a crystal chandelier rising up from the overhead in the officers' wardroom, and the first crew—the precise Germans—living as ghosts in some time warp aboard the jumbled "glory of the German fleet."

I looked at the horizon and back down. That quickly my father was out of sight. I waited, beginning to worry how long was too long.

Three things went up in the living room next: a knife with a bone handle and a metal sheath; a round wall barometer, face and glass missing and the brass plating frosted with corrosion; and a U.S. Army C ration that even my father was afraid to open.

Jack wouldn't leave the stuff alone, fingering it or holding it up to look at. He had honed the eight-inch knife, sheathed it in the holder, and attached that to his belt.

My mother threatened to shovel everything outside. "He never does anything in a normal way," she told me. "It's always the extreme with him. The man's obsessed."

That night my father went to Com-Closed, and I followed a little later. I was hoping Beebe would show up, even though I always acted as if I didn't notice. Something was churning, but I didn't know what to make of him. Everyone seemed to respect Joe Beebe. I'd seen him head off a brawl between a couple of aviators once, just by a look, not even words.

At Com-Closed I found my father talking the ears off a couple of petty officers who couldn't get away. He had the knife out on the table and two water glasses of Mars Okinawa whiskey lined up in front of him. Doc was sitting at the end of the table, dozing, his hands up on his head. Skeeter had a chair of his own and was eating soggy peanuts and drinking beer from his own special cup, kept hung on a hook at the bar.

My father was telling a story he'd heard about Larry Roach, a Princeton boy, a scientist who had been there for the

testing eight years before. He'd wanted to study the impact of
the bomb, ironically, on the cockroach population aboard
the blasted ships. My father was laughing so hard that he
could barely talk. Tears were in his eyes. "There's Roach
belowdeck collecting jars of his relatives," he said. "Then
the poor SOB drops a jar, and he's knee-deep in hot roaches
climbing up his legs. Big suckers, too. A whole new breed.
They're as big as him and twice as smart. Motherfucking
Christ, did he ever get crazier than a shithouse rat."

I noticed Joe Beebe and another pilot, Budd Barnett—
"Buzzard"—playing eight ball in the back. I got a ginger ale
and went over by the jukebox near them, pretending to scan
the list even though I knew it all by heart: "High Noon,"
"Stardust," "Tennessee Waltz," "Woody Woodpecker,"
"Some Enchanted Evening," "Crazy Man Crazy."

Beebe was studying a shot, and Buzzard was giving him
a hard time about being too slow. "Not a game of speed,"
Beebe said. "Got to figure your angle of attack, angle of
incidence."

Buzzard chomped on an apple as Beebe clipped an orange
striped ball with the cue and sank two others into pockets.
He concentrated on chalking the stick and stared Buzzard
down. Then he looked at me. " 'Angle of incidence' is at the
point when enough air hits your wing for liftoff."

I nodded. I liked the sound of 'angle of incidence'—
smart, precise, important. How I thought Joe Beebe talked.
But the words made me think of something more menacing
like objects on a collision course.

I could hear my father's voice across the bar, describing
one of the tests as if he'd been there. Everyone had taken off,
and only Junie, the bartender, was listening.

"Had to sandbag the shore and dig into a ditch, sweating

like bastards." I'd heard Herschel Peck, one of Jack's friends, tell the story. My father propped his head up with his hand, steadying it. "Waiting for countdown, wondering if the whole fucking island's going to go up. Then the flash hits. Now I swear this. You could see your own skeleton. God-damn son of a bitchenest thing. Your own fricking bones X-rayed. Imagine that, Junie. Look down and see your bony toes through your boondockers." Jack glanced down at his arms and legs as if he were seeing through his skin. Junie leaned on the bar with his elbows and shook his head as if he were hearing this for the first time.

"The lagoon blows up, see?" my father went on. "Niag-ara Falls backwards and a billion times bigger. Then the tidal wave swamps the ships like they're paper matches. Melts down their masts. Meanwhile, everyone's bouncing around like they're on a sprung bed with a two-bit whore."

Sometimes my father talked as if it were one big party out there. He'd heard that the men would get stinking drunk after each shot.

"Your pop ever get tired of that crap?" Joe Beebe said, offering me the stick to try a shot. I noticed the shocks of gray in his black hair and the dark stubble on his face. His pale green eyes looked as if they were designed for camouflage.

"What's it to you?" I said.

"He better not be crawling on hot ships anymore. That's all. Crazy if he is."

"There's nothing wrong with my father." I looked straight at him.

"He lives in his alky lies."

"Who asked you anyway?" I turned to walk away, and he grabbed the belt around my shorts and jerked me toward him. It pinched my waist until he let go.

"Stay away from that ship. I know what I'm talking about," he said. "You listening to me?"

"I've got ears." I twisted around and strutted away. The whole time I was conscious of how I looked from the back as if I could look anything like Betty Grable. I wanted Joe Beebe to come after me and apologize for what he'd said about my father, but he didn't. He went back to the pool game. I could say things about my old man, but I didn't want anyone else to.

It's not that I didn't consider what Beebe said about the *Eugen.* If anyone would know about it, he would. But I thought he was being overly cautious. A stand on radiation had always been vague. Men wore film badges to measure the roentgens they were exposed to, but it was after the fact. And the military kept upping the count that was safe anyway. Most people weren't dropping dead yet.

I sat down with my father. I could tell his alcohol high was turning to deep depression. Jack had a watery, lost look in his eyes. He was still talking to Junie, even though Junie had the water running and couldn't really hear him.

"Mike, sweetest guy, just snapped out there," my father said. "Started pounding this ensign over nothing. Some stupid argument about a pitcher at a Yankees game. Flash does something to the brain, seeing a shot every week. It does something to a man. One guy dug a grave and buried himself. Someone had to shovel him out."

Sometimes when my old man didn't think I was close enough to hear, he'd tell another story. I was right there next to him this night, but he told it anyway.

"I hear some guys went so crackbrained they put a skirt on a monkey and lined up to screw her." Jack looked over at Skeeter in the chair, holding up a peanut and putting it in his mouth. "My God."

★ ★ ★

Early the next day my father got his scuba gear ready. I threw on my clothes and caught him on the back patio. "Let's not go today. Why don't we just skip it, Daddy?" I said.

My father didn't bother to respond. He finished off a beer and headed to the truck. I followed. "Why don't you stay behind this time?" he snapped. He clanged the tanks in the back and started up the engine. I jumped in. "You ever think I might want to be alone?" he said. I didn't answer. In fact, we didn't say anything on the way to the dock or out to the *Eugen.*

My father was moving slowly after we reached the ship. His shoulders drooped when he put on the tanks. He descended the ladder stiffly, like an old man easing into a hot bath. "Adios," he said lightly as if to make up for his bad mood earlier.

"Bombs over Tokyo," I said.

I felt sorry for him suddenly in that fizzle of bubbles. When I was eleven I'd felt sorry for him and mad. He'd had to go into the hospital to dry out. It was coming again. I could see it.

That time in the hospital he gave me a kit of beads from the Navy exchange. His hands were shaking so much from the DTs that he spilled the box when he handed it to me. Bright wooden beads bounced across the floor, and he tried to pick them up.

I wanted to cry for his bedroom slippers that he kept falling out of, the bent-up toes, and the way he hugged me so hard that I thought my ribs would pop. But when he kissed me good-bye, I wiped his spit off my face, hard against my sleeve. I hated that it had to be this way. Even then I knew it would always be this way, and nothing I could do would ever change it.

★ ★ ★

When my father didn't come back within an hour, I pictured
him clawing at an iron door slammed shut in the *Eugen* or
lost in the passageways, disoriented as a deepwater fish upside
down in darkness.

Go for help, I thought. But there wasn't time to go to
Kwaj.

Rust on the ship looked thick as mink pelts. As the tide
lowered, I could see more of the wreck through mottled
light. On the lip of a porthole hung a chair, the back bubbled
from the sun and the rest a seat of mussels.

I knew my father had entered by the bridge, was going
along the port side, and in through a hatch that would take
him to the crew's quarters. Below him were ceiling lights
with red glass covers, bunks wrenched from the walls like
tossed dominoes. Razor-edged clams riveted the arched bulk-
head openings to the officers' country. The huge dining table
was suspended upside down, no light catching in the crystal
of any chandelier.

Near the bottom of the wreck there were turrets and
antiaircraft guns, torpedoes ready to fire, lodged in their
tubes. The superstructure would be smashed to tin foil, like
a smelted dime I'd seen from the pocket of a pilot. He'd
survived a power line, but his flight suit had burned off him
and the coin melted flat, evaporating the imprint of Mercury.

I looked in the water and tried to see my father down
in the wreck. Fish darted between coral stacked in brilliant
pillars. I waited one minute. One more minute.

I checked the tank, the pressure gauge, and began suiting
up. I put on the harness and weight belt and tightened the
straps, slipped into fins and defogged the mask. To test the
mouthpiece I bit down on the nodules until I thought my
teeth would loosen in their sockets.

I had to believe he'd be back before I was done. I didn't know if anything could make me go in there. By rote, I went through the maneuvers: Submerge the regulator and press the mouthpiece to test it; equalize pressure in your ears; clear the hoses.

Another minute. I counted to sixty in one thousands. One more minute. Once I saw a drunk sailor jump off a dock and never surface. People watched, waiting while he drowned. He was already stiff by the time they found him, his white legs rigid as a mannequin's when they brought him over the side of the boat.

I imagined my father. Each second was counting now.

Suddenly he was there beside the *Eugen*. He spit out his mouthpiece and sucked in air, gasping and coughing. Jack struggled with something in his hands that weighed him down as he kicked over to the *Delores Ann*. I helped him as he heaved the load up on the rung of the ladder.

My hands slipped over the slime and barnacle covering. The object was a bell, the size of a small lampshade. I clawed at the surface until I found the rim and then pulled it up.

My father's eyes looked glazed and wild behind the mask.

"I was scared to death. What happened to you?" I said before he even got up the ladder. He stepped in, panting, and grabbed a towel. It was a moment before he could speak.

"You see the bell? Isn't it something?" He was still catching his breath. "Son of a bitch was stuck under some barrels." He finally noticed I had on gear. "How come you're suited up?"

"I was going after you."

"What are you talking about?" as if I were crazy. He got his tanks off and cracked open a beer. "You can't dive." He threw his fins against the side of the boat.

"You expect me not to do anything? You were about out of air." I started pulling my gear off and clanging it down.

"I was fine. I can take care of myself, okay? No problem." He rolled the bell around on its rim, inspecting it. The algae and slime covering looked like fur, like Skeeter's monkey hair. My father worked some of it off with his fingernail. "Brass." Then suddenly he yelled out, "Jesus Christ. It's got the goddamn eagle and swastika engraved in it." He held it up to me. "Look at that." I could see a few deeply etched lines of the eagle. "Well, I'll be a son of a bitch," he said, and went back to cleaning it. "Your old man brought up the prize of a lifetime."

I went over to his tanks and checked the pressure gauge. The needle was at a critical point in the red zone. He wouldn't have lasted much longer down there. I wanted to smack him for doing this to both of us.

"That bell worth risking your life for?" I asked.

He was rubbing the bell with a towel and didn't answer. Then he leaned back against an orange cushion and smoked his cigarette. The white towel in his hand was covered with strands of the mossy slime. "Get off my back," he said. "Everything was under control, I told you."

"Yeah? Well, I think you screwed up. You were diving drunk, and you ran out of air down there fooling with that stupid thing. You could have gotten yourself killed."

He glowered at me. "I don't need a smart-mouth kid telling me what to do." He stabbed at each word with the cigarette in his hand.

I glared back at him, at the drops of water on his chest and shoulders, the beer bottle stuck in one hand, and the towel and cigarette in the other. "So go ahead and kill yourself," I yelled. "Nothing I can do about it." I hung over the side of the boat and shouted, "The hell with this crap."

As soon as we got to Kwaj, I took off for home. My father didn't come back.

"I'm fed up with trying to fight him," Matty said. She'd dumped the *Eugen* artifacts out behind the patio. I didn't tell her what had happened that day.

My mother began moving the furniture around. She'd do that or scrub tile grout sometimes when she felt trapped. The house was immaculate every day, and the furniture usually rearranged.

Later that night I went to Com-Closed. I came in the back so my father wouldn't spot me right off. I could see him and Doc, my father going on about something. Skeeter was passed out on the floor next to his cup.

Joe Beebe came up behind me as soon as I walked in. Someone had punched in Patti Page's "Tennessee Waltz," and Beebe grabbed me to dance. He was still holding a pool cue in one hand when we swirled around a small clearing.

"Guess I shouldn't have said anything about your old man last night," Beebe said. "I was worried."

"Forget it," I said. I didn't tell him he'd been right about my father.

It was hot, even with the air conditioner going. Crescent moons of sweat stained Beebe's blue shirt. He smelled like citronella. I didn't look at him, even when he took glances at me. On turns I could see my father watching us. After the song my old man had Junie bring over a cream soda for me and a beer for Beebe. Then Jack did something else that made me think he was going to ease up on Joe Beebe for my sake.

He called over to him in a friendly voice and told us to come to his table.

When we walked over, I could see the bell sitting there on the green plastic tabletop. It had been cleaned so the brass almost shone. The crown where it had been attached was ripped as if the bell had wrenched loose during a blast and hurtled down a corridor.

My father rolled the bell toward Beebe. The clapper was split in half. "Look at this bastard," my father said, pointing to the Nazi emblem. He was shit-faced. "We'd a been kraut-made, too, if they had their way, right, ace?" My father and Doc roared at that. Beebe was waiting to see where this was leading. Jack looked up at him. "Lucky helped bring this beaut up. Right, you old sweet thing?"

"Come on, Daddy." I shook my head.

He put his arm around my waist. "Got it off the *Eugen,* ace. What do you think of that?" With one hand, my father picked up the bell by the torn crown and clanged it, daring Beebe more with each clap. "Sons a bitch has only got a half-ass bang." Jack kept ringing it. "Well? You want to squawk, ace?"

"You're a fool, Jack," Beebe said.

"Yeah, tell it, sport," my father answered.

"Least you could do is think about your daughter," Beebe said.

"My daughter's none of your business. She's in a lot more danger around you."

"That damn thing's contaminated." Beebe's voice rose. "It's radioactive. What in the hell's wrong with you?"

My father upped the ante with a louder voice. "I don't care about the fricking bell. I'm telling you, keep your hands off my daughter." Everyone in the place looked up. I stared down a couple of officers grinning like hyenas at a nearby table.

"Go sleep it off," Beebe said to my old man.

"I might be in my cups, but I'm not blind," Jack said.

"Come on, Jack," Doc said, too drunk to really read the situation. "Don't be sore at the kid. Joe, sit down and drink your beer."

"Radiation exposure," Beebe said to both of them, resting his hands on the back of a chair and leaning into the table. "Doesn't that mean something to you?"

"I've lived through a hell of a lot more than a little bit of that fallout shit," my father said. "Go back to your pool game."

"You're fucking crazy," Beebe said, shaking his head. My father held up his drink as if in a toast. Beebe slammed a chair out of his way, and without saying anything to me, he walked out.

"You've got a bad mouth, kid," my father called after him. "Stay away from my daughter, you hear me?" The place went quiet except for the rattle of dice on the Formica bar.

"Stop it," I yelled at my father. "Just stop it."

"Ace's just trying to get in your pants," my father said. "I know him. He's a snake." My father's face was red from sunburn and drinking. I could see broken veins in his nose.

"And you're a drunk," I said. "Nothing's going to change." He looked startled and reeled back in slow motion, as if he'd been hit by a punch underwater. "I hate it," I said. "I can't stand watching it."

"God damn you. You're talking to your old man. Show some respect, kid." He knocked the table with his elbow, making the drinks slosh and the bottle wobble.

Someone punched in "Stardust" on the jukebox. My

father grabbed a book of soggy matches from the puddle of whiskey and tried to light up. I noticed that the sharp creases my mother always pressed into his shirt were gone. The khaki looked damp and sour, and the short sleeves that usually flared smartly were wrinkled.

"Sit down. You're making me nervous," he barked.

I didn't move.

"Suit yourself," he said, and looked away.

Skeeter stretched in his sleep and gently wrapped his long dark fingers around Doc's chair leg. I stood there, not knowing why I hadn't walked out by then.

Suddenly Joe Beebe swung open the bar door. He headed toward us, cutting through the chairs. He was carrying something in his hand. My father sobered for a moment when he spotted him. "Now what the hell's he want?"

It looked like a small silver toolbox, but Beebe was carrying a Geiger counter.

"Get the fuck out of here, you louse," my father said.

Beebe stepped closer and pointed the instrument at the bell. A crackle like static from a radio increased to a keening as it picked up the roentgens. Everyone in the club, the officers and wives, even a man slumped at the bar, turned to watch. They came over to the table and stood a few feet away.

"It's hot, for Godsake. Get rid of it," Beebe said.

"Geiger counter will do that near metal," my father said. "It don't mean shit." He flicked his cigarette.

Junie walked over, holding a bar rag. "What's going on, Jack?"

"This pissant's giving me a hard time," my father said, pointing at Beebe.

"He's got contaminated material. It's got to go. Now," Beebe said, motioning toward the bell. There was another shriek of blurred clicks as he moved the detector in that direction.

"I know what the hell's going on," my father said. "I know more about the shots than the guys who been there." He took a drink and then looked around at everyone watching him and listening to the static.

"Come on, let's get out of here," Doc said to my father.

"Hell, no." My father slapped his hand down on the wet table. "Beebe's not running me off."

Beebe turned to Junie. "I'm telling you, it's got to be dealt with."

"Hey, you got something to say, say it to me," my father said, standing up. "Stinking brown-nosing son of a bitch. You think you're goddamn better than me?"

Beebe turned off the detector and sat it carefully on the table. "I think you drank yourself loco, Jack. You don't know any better than to fry yourself and expose her and everyone else."

My father held onto the table to steady himself. Suddenly he stood and lunged, slugging Beebe, missing part of his face but catching enough of his lip to bloody it. Beebe absorbed the punch; it hardly jostled him. Someone gasped, and a lieutenant moved toward Beebe, ready to hold him back, but Beebe didn't go after my father. He rubbed his lip and looked at the blood on his hand.

"You're killing yourself, old man," Beebe said calmly. He grabbed the detector and flipped it on. Then he came right up to my father and moved the instrument in a long line from Jack's throat down to his legs. Only the high-pitched crackling could be heard in the bar. My father didn't move at first. He held up his hand as if to shield himself. When he finally took a step back, he made a wild swipe at the machine. His hand whacked the box.

"Get out of here, you dirty bastard," Jack yelled, and held his hand as if he were in pain. "Get away from me."

Beebe turned off the Geiger counter. When he met my eyes, he looked past me, ashamed, knowing he'd gone too far. He pushed through the ring of people and was gone suddenly.

"I'm fine," my father said, looking down at himself. "Never felt better in my life." But he held his arms out away from his body as if he were covered in manure. Everyone stepped back farther from him. I wanted to go up and protect him from this, but I saw what was around him.

I found Joe Beebe sitting on the beach a few minutes later and startled him when I sat down.

"Put it up to me," I said.

"What?"

"Hold the Geiger counter up to me. Do it."

"Just forget it, LeeAnn. You don't want to know."

"Maybe I do."

"There's nothing you can do about it anyway. For-get it."

"I can't forget. I want to know." I considered grabbing it from him right then and switching it on. I didn't. I knew it would follow me. I thought I could control fear by worrying it through. But fear always circled out larger.

"Everything is going to be okay," he said. "It's all right."

He put his arm around me, and I let him because I needed it, even though I knew I should hate him for what he had done to my father. I felt a sick-in-my-stomach feeling for my father, thinking of him in Com-Closed, set apart from everyone there, as alien as he'd ever felt. My father scrambling under a hospital bed for those beads when I was eleven, grabbing me so hard I thought my bones would snap like kindling.

I stayed with Joe Beebe on the beach that night. I moved against his arm so that we fell backward. I didn't breathe until I finally had to gasp for the humid air. He turned me toward him. We lay there, looking up into a sky as expansive as the ocean around that small island. He pushed against me, and I moved with him.

It was one o'clock by the fluorescent dial on his watch, closing time at Com-Closed. Within moments I heard my father pass by us less than fifty feet away. The bell in his hand clanged with each unsteady step home.

Starting from E

Nineteen seventy-eight, Majuro. Because it was nearly Christmas, silver tinsel had been draped along with leis over the side of the open coffin at the airport. The Marshall Islander was laid out in his best—cheap American clothes he'd be sweltering in if alive: rayon pants, white nylon shirt, a tie. Leis of frangipani and magenta bougainvillea looped his neck. Around the head, a woven band with tiny white shells that women collect on a treeless, deserted island. A pair of plastic sunglasses over his eyes. One stem was held in place with a paper clip.

Scar at the man's neck: thyroid removed, radiation exposure, twenty-five thousand dollars' compensation from the U.S.

Disfranchised men, broad women in long dresses, their babies, children gathered around the plywood coffin set on a waiting bench. Below it a rooster crowed inside a fruit crate, and a boy with metallic blue Christmas tree tinsel tied around one pant leg poked a twig at the bird. Bing Crosby's "White Christmas" was playing over the speaker.

Twenty-four years since I'd been in the Marshalls. "Keep your good intentions in California," Joe Beebe had told me when I wanted to come out to the islands a few months before.

"Just what the Marshallese need—another American, one more *ribelle*. Forget the paint-by-numbers liberalism. It's too complicated, too late, Lee." It hadn't sounded like him.

Later I wondered if he meant too late for the Marshalls or himself. Expatriate troublemaking journalist over the years, he'd laid open what the military and DOE didn't want told: accounts of the blasts and cover-ups, levels of radiation exposure to the islanders and military, the medical problems, his own cancer. He'd passed on information to congressional committees. Some people had wanted him muzzled. It would be done for them.

I hadn't known how sick Beebe was when he asked me to handle his affairs if anything happened. Something did. Now I was left with his odd request: his ashes split among his women—his daughter and her Bikinian mother and his ex-wife, Marlene, in the States. Marlene still had the ashes of her first husband, Jerry—Beebe's buddy. Beebe thought it would be fearful symmetry for her to have both husbands on her mantel like bookends.

"What the hell," he'd said to me, laughing. "Do it or don't. Include yourself if you like. Whatever makes sense."

I could hear ice clinking in a drink, all the way from the Marshalls to California, in spite of the delayed response and static from our voices traveling under the Pacific. With medication and booze, Beebe sounded like some sloppy drunk he'd despise.

Division did make sense. Beebe's whole life had been divided, fractured between intentions, women. Fighter pilot.

Later flying recon and Air-Sea Rescue during the nuclear tests. Then his dissent from the military.

In Honolulu, where Beebe's body had been shipped for cremation, I ended up with all of him, unlike what happened in life. In a black vinyl bag I carried the white container, heavy cardboard, a size bigger than a corsage box, dense as ore. Dazed by my baggage, I left immediately for the Marshalls.

How to explain Beebe's plan to his daughter, Libby, and her mother, May, was a question. May had taken care of Beebe when he was sick. The day he died, she probably laid him down on pandanus mats and washed him with special leaves, Marshallese custom to preserve a body in the heat. Cremation wasn't done here. You buried family, sometimes in the front yard.

I didn't know how we'd even do this thing. Maybe with a teaspoon and a small set of scales to measure out our amounts, for the good Beebe brought us, for the bullshit we went through.

I was en route to May and Libby on Ebeye to deliver part of him. But first to ponder my share on E island. Enubuj, an uninhabited islet with World War II debris, where Beebe and I used to go in 1954.

Out of the window of my plane to Kwaj, I saw a pilot and a mechanic unbolting three pair of seats from a prop plane to fit in the Marshallese man's coffin, the boxes of chickens and roosters, and a baby pig on a leash about to be crated. The pilot, probably a newcomer, shook his head, not understanding the operative word out here is "adjustments." You learn to make them.

Men carried the closed coffin on their shoulders to the bush plane. The plane seats were lined up on the tarmac one behind the other, and the boy with tinsel bounced on one as if he were headed somewhere.

Swarms of terns shrieked as I tied up a small motorboat on E the next day, twenty minutes from Kwajalein, near the wrecked *Prinz Eugen,* where my father used to dive.

Kwaj was an Army-owned missile range now. Dummy nuclear warheads launched from California are slam-dunked into the lagoon at ten thousand miles an hour. Bomb- and dope-sniffing German shepherds inspect luggage at the base airport.

I couldn't stay on Kwaj any more than the islanders who worked there, so I took the ferry over to Ebeye and rented the boat to get to E.

Mosquitoes were thick on E in the muggy afternoon. Through the years Beebe had come here to scuba dive. Grasses and vines grew over the remains of a concrete gun emplacement. Ditched in a breadfruit tree was an unraveled cassette tape.

Only one resident now: a timid black pig that limped from polio, a reminder of Beebe's own bum leg peppered with shrapnel during the war.

There was still a sunken spot in the ground for the well Beebe had dug in 1954 and filled in again. He'd shoveled down to the lens of rainwater layered over the coral. We used to bring up water in a bucket on a rope for the *tiwtiw,* the Marshallese bath, luxury in the humidity and our ritual before returning to Kwaj. We'd splash down, soap, rinse off.

It was during the last seven months before my family was transferred from Kwaj in late '54 that Joe Beebe and I would escape to E in a glass-bottom boat. When he could sneak off, Beebe would walk by my house, singing, "Come along and follow me, to the bottom of the sea."

The boat had been made over from the fuselage of a scrapped small plane. Beebe and some buddies had torched out a square, set in a plate of glass, and raised the whole thing up on pontoons.

A small concrete hut on E was cool in the tropical swelter, and Beebe and I made it our home in the afternoons. We'd spread down a parachute to lie together. The sun of a spent Japanese flag hung before us on one wall.

We had found the flag shoved into a crack in the foundation of the hut. "To the defeat of Nippon," Beebe had said, tacking it up our first day on E. We toasted to our take-over with shots of George Dickel. A day later we started setting up housekeeping.

I strung frangipani for leis and tried to plait pandanus leaves into a skirt like those the early Marshallese women wore. Sometimes I put on a Hawaiian grass skirt. He liked the rustle of grass when I'd jerk the tie at my waist and let it drop from my hips. I'd hide the grasses in his pants pockets so he'd find them later, working their way through his cotton pocket linings.

In the afternoon heat I waved a Marshallese fan of sea turtle shell over us. The fan was an idea I'd taken from a nude painting in his quarters on Kwaj—Beebe's estranged wife, Marlene, living in the States. They had split up after only three months in 1950 but were still married. Beebe had just told me about her that summer of 1954. Marlene, turned on her side, a red Oriental fan up to her face, the curve of her hip like a glorious sun rising.

The concrete of the little block hut was wearing down now, pitted from the rains. I was afraid to go in the building. The Japanese flag we'd hung up was gone. Rain puddles on the floor spread to the back.

I had never lost contact with Beebe since I left Kwaj. I'd

lived with two men, each for several years, but never married. Sometimes I asked Beebe for advice about men. Like asking a thief how to protect my house, I told him.

"Forget men. They're all dicks anyway," he'd said for years. "Do something yourself. Get out of the self-indulgence."

"You condescending son of a bitch," I'd said to him. Our relationship had evolved over the years.

But he was right that my life had lurched recklessly, without fixed direction. I traveled around as an indefinite student, kept afloat in part-time jobs, transferred out of places as if I were still in the military. I would pack up the car and pull out at dawn with a Thermos of coffee, believing in the promise of the next temporary station. Expectations as vivid as the scenes in old highway billboards: families waving from snake farms or motel pool slides.

I made my homes into islands, containment in uncertain vastness. Places became bases where I expected orders.

On E, I lit mosquito coils and put them around me. I opened a jar of dried beef and ate some with crackers.

Later I fell asleep and woke to a rat licking my leg. Its cool cordlike tail slipped over my ankle as I screamed.

I lit a candle and opened a beer, stepped into the lagoon and dipped out water with a cup, soaping and washing. It was a simple pleasure standing alone in the muggy heat, listening to "Moonlight Cocktail" on tape, the black pig— my uncomplicated date—looking on shyly.

I set up a net hammock between palm trees and settled in, holding the box. Below me the pig stuck its snout into an opened coconut shell. In the quiet night it was just the sound of the pig's teeth scraping out the meat.

That night I invited the dead in. I asked for a sign,

something to materialize, something to move. Nothing did. I said it was urgent.

"Come to E if you summon the *cojones*, pal." "Urgent" written on an envelope I sent through the island mail in 1954. Enclosed were powdery imprints of my breasts, dipped in rouge and stamped on creamy stationery. I was seventeen.

As I soaped his leg in the *tiwtiw* on E, I could feel the chain of Japanese souvenirs under the slick suds on his calf. The latest about McCarthy was coming over the shortwave that day in 1954. Back in the States, people were watching the Senate hearings on the small green screens of their big, boxy televisions as they ate TV dinners, the latest novelty.

Time was running out. My father was going to be transferred back to the States in two months, and I'd be shipped out also. That day I brought it up, the notion of the two of us. Waiting for someone to make up his mind about you is time better spent in a coma, I had decided.

I roped my hair around Beebe's ankle and raised it up his leg. "So what's your mental thinking about the future down the road? What do you visually see happening?" We used to mimic a major on Kwaj who'd speak in redundancies.

Beebe reached over to snap off a pandanus pod from a tree. Clusters of the pods looked like giant grenades and tasted like an overly sweet fruity Daiquiri with a nauseating aftertaste.

"Are you worried?" He chewed on the stringy golden fruit and shook his head. "Honest to God. I don't know what's going to happen. One thing I do know. You don't deserve to get hurt, sugah, by an old wreck like me."

He tried to conceal his southern accent, but it got

stronger when he was tired. He'd say things like "I'll call on you 'round suppatime."

I tied the grass skirt around me and then picked at a splinter I'd taken in from the ammo box we used as a dinner table. That day the wooden crate had been set with a white tablecloth, silverware, wineglasses I'd brought from home.

Beebe tossed the fruit off into the bushes and wrapped a towel around his waist. "If you've got to worry, sweet pea, I'll tell you something to worry about—that troublemaking lummox McCarthy or getting food to the Bikinians." He turned up the shortwave.

The Bikini Islanders had been moved to Kili and weren't much better off now than when they'd suffered malnutrition on Rongerik. What was really on my mind constantly, though, wasn't the islanders or McCarthy; it was Beebe and what would happen to us. Compared with the suffering of the Marshallese, this was unmentionable. But I was scared. I was beginning to decide that there were only one, two, maybe three people you could love fiercely in a life, and I was using up one of those times with Joe Beebe.

I watched as he frothed up a cake of soap with his shave brush as if he were peaking whipped cream. The dark hair on his chest looked like a plaque of fur. He stood there in the white towel looking into a mirror nailed on a branch and asked if I wanted to go along on a supply ship in a week to Kili. Beebe had a preoccupation with the Bikinians since he'd been involved with the evacuation eight years before. I didn't know what was behind it. I was about to find out.

"You're doing everything you can for them," I told him.

"It's not enough." I laughed at his soap-whitened face, but he didn't think anything was funny. He drew the straight edge over his jaw in clean, precise strokes.

Most men I knew on Kwaj just had a brassy front, a

fuck-it or fight-it code. They'd log their free time at the Snake Pit, the bachelors' bar, and for a hoot get shit-faced and Houdini someone—rope a willing sap to a junked cockpit seat and throw him off the dock.

Joe Beebe was above those stunts. He seemed to hold himself personally accountable for circumstances with the islanders. The Lone Ranger. I still saw him that way. Then he told me.

"I've got responsibilities on Kili. My seven-year-old daughter, Libby."

This was the first I'd heard of his daughter. But during the evacuation of Bikini in '46, I had seen him with May, a young native woman.

"If you want to see the future, I'm not leaving the islands," he said. "Even when my time's over."

"It doesn't matter to me. I'll stay, too." For years I'd been dying to get off "the rock," and now suddenly I was saying I wanted to be in this place that I couldn't even begin to describe to people back in the States.

"I'm fourteen years older, doll. You've got to get out of here, go to college, do something."

"I don't care about college. I don't care about out *there*." I thought of us as a family, what my own family was not. "Ask me to stay."

He wiped a towel over his face. "When are you going to realize it was my fault leading you into this like every fucking thing else I've led people into?"

"I see it."

"Didn't your old man ever teach you when to tell some bastard to shove off?"

"I don't want you to shove off."

"You made me into something I'm not, for Godsake."

"I want to be with you. I thought you wanted that."

His hand blazed a course up the grasses of the skirt, over my leg. I grabbed his hand. "Why didn't you tell me about your daughter?"

He didn't answer me.

Alone on E, I tried to open the box again the next day, but I couldn't bring myself to lift the lid.

I'd read about excavations of ancient burials. Coupling skeletons found in a field, speared together forever during someone's jealous raging. Handmaidens buried with a queen, hair ribbons turned to powder over their smashed skulls. One girl without a ribbon. She must have removed the bow from her hair, knowing what was to come. Just a trace of ribbon now, in the outline of her pocket.

No last story in a box of ashes, dust from a nuclear frontier town. Ironically, my father wouldn't die of cancer, damned if he'd let Joe Beebe be right about the effects of radiation. I didn't know about myself.

In the last years Beebe had told me what he'd learned about the testing cover-ups. Some I'd read about later in a book. At a Nevada test site in the fifties, soldiers stumbled on a compound where men had been locked inside, electrodes attached to them, hair gone, skin peeling from a blast. The military tried to brainwash the soldiers into believing they had never seen men being used as test animals hundreds of yards from ground zero. The men in the compound probably transients—drunks, junkies picked up on the road, unknowns with no history. Like the Marshallese, nobody's son, father, or brother, no one to trace them to this place in hell. There were no limits, here or there. Anything could be tolerated, accommodated, so we could make room for more.

My father had wanted to be in the middle of the nuclear

test ground. But he'd numbered our days on Kwaj, etching a hash mark inside the bathroom medicine chest every morning, each stroke a count against the days left. Seven hundred lines by the time we left the Marshalls. We went forward day after day of each rusty scratch, forced to see things we didn't want to see.

That year when I was seventeen, I would leave home, leave my attempt of it on E. In spite of what was here, I was afraid to go.

On E now, I opened a warm, foamy beer, then set the box on the shore and waded into the water. Small jellyfish stung like nettles; their cloudy sky blue tentacles brought up welts on my legs. I looked back at the islet, the box that I couldn't open.

It wasn't a plan of action but loneliness that would drive me off E. The next day was Christmas Eve, and I wasn't going to do this alone.

I was starved for normalcy, life and humor, but Ebeye, "ghetto of the Pacific," wasn't the place for it. Eight thousand people lived on one tenth of a square mile.

I got a small ratty motel room with one fan and water bugs the size of matchbook toy trucks. After stashing my things I left quickly, taking the bag with me. Outside a room, a small group of Marshallese women and men were gathered, listening through a window to someone's shortwave.

Things fell apart out here and didn't get fixed. Sometimes human waste gurgled out of the sink drains. One end of the island was a garbage dump, a trembling mosaic of flies and a smell that could level anything near. Families lived in shacks next to the dump. Through the garbage and rats, kids played baseball with a stick and pieces of cardboard for mitts. Women bent over a campfire nearby, cooking fish.

In an alley a group of teenagers shot craps. Boys set up a rooster fight, betting dimes and nickels. Drunk men yelled out to me.

By the lagoon people were butchering a hog for Christmas. The carcass was strung up on a pole over the water, and a red cloud pooled below.

Old recordings of Christmas songs, "Here Comes Santa Claus" and "Jingle Bells," played constantly from a loudspeaker, blasting out music to the town. An old woman sitting on the ground outside a shack dumped detergent into half a suitcase, used as a basin, and scrubbed clothes on a small piece of plywood.

I wasn't ready to give up the box yet, but I went to the Ebeye clinic, where Libby worked, to catch a glimpse of her. In 1954, when I went to Kili with Beebe, I saw her at first in the thatched schoolhouse for a celebration welcoming the supply ship. Smoky green eyes turned down on the ends like Beebe's, lanky arms and legs, auburn shoulder-length hair that hung straight. She was drinking from an evaporated milk can, the top a jagged disk still hinged to the can.

Islanders on Kili had sat on the floor of the schoolhouse or stood outside looking through the windows to watch the Americans. Beebe and I sat with the king and queen of the island at the only table in the room. Leis had been draped around our necks, and *alus*—shell-decorated bands—placed on our heads like crowns, as if we were royalty.

At the Ebeye clinic this late afternoon, there was no one at the front desk, just a wastebasket to catch rain that leaked from the roof. I walked down the hall, looking into rooms with chipped paint and World War II metal beds.

I left the clinic and headed for a local dive, for a drink, for company. The place was a mix of Peace Corps workers, young missionaries, military men from Kwaj, islanders. In the corner of the room a band was doing a sorry version of "San Antonio Rose." Walls of the bar had been painted turquoise. Tilted in one corner was a flocked white Christmas tree, hung with shiny Christmas balls and halved coconut shells spray-painted gold. Each coconut held a tiny nativity scene with robed matchstick figures.

I had a couple of beers before I got the nerve to talk to an older guy in white jeans and a polo shirt. Ray, clean-cut, gray hair, looked like a State Department type.

I noticed a navigational stick chart hung up behind us, a traditional guide the islanders had used in the past to sail between islands. Flat wooden sticks showed the currents and the islands, marked by gold-ringer shells. I pulled Ray over to the chart and pointed out Enubuj and Kwaj and the two sticks bowed in an oblong shape around them, plotting the swells. He examined the map, touching the slick shells. After a couple of drinks he could even be a poor replica of Joe Beebe from the side.

"We could go there," he said. "What do you think?"

I didn't answer him, but I bought the next round, and we stepped outside. It was almost twilight. Across the street a celebration was starting at the church. Families were arriving on foot with their kids in homemade outfits: teenage girls in matching shifts, boys in matching shirts.

"Marshallese kids do dances at Christmas," I told Ray. "For *jepta*." I was only parroting what Beebe had told me. He'd sent pictures of Libby in the audience at a *jepta*. She was glancing across her shoulder, smiling at him.

The band started up a butchered version of "Blue Christmas." We tried to dance, squeezed between the tables inside. Drinks ran under our feet. The guitarist went into a solo of

"O Holy Night." Some of the people in the bar were singing along, standing in a winding line between the tables and chairs, waving their glasses. An unexpected moment.

From the Christmas tree the matchstick figures watched out of their nativities. Below them, the earth diorama and its victims and saviors, sweating out their stories, their destinies in the Marshalls. Beebe was swinging on my arm, baggage for the last train to E.

Outside, more islanders were heading toward the celebration. Radios were synchronized to the only station on the island. I went to the door and stood watching a family walking into the church, the parents and three children, a baby in the mother's arms.

The band started up again, competing with music from the church and a speaker on the street roaring "Feliz Navidad." Without turning around to Ray, I wandered out into the street and the crowd toward the celebration.

Off behind someone's shack in dim light was a small group of men, one pounding a stringy mass over a stone, then pouring water over it. Ponape pepper root, pulverized for the *sakau,* a mild numbing narcotic. Legend had it that *sakau* came from the injured foot of a ghost. The man wrung out the juice of the root into a coconut half and passed it around.

Alongside the church teenagers were lined up to practice their dances, stomping and clapping in lines. Shutters were off the open windows and the wide doors left open so the church was like a huge patio. I stepped up to a window to watch.

Inside, a group shuffled through steps, the young teenagers still with some hope. The girls bright in new dresses, conscious of each move and everyone watching. Smells of sweet perfumes and coconut oil on their skin and hair.

Families stood around, some holding infants up on the

sills of the windows to see inside. Kids ran in between the dancers. A boy outside pushed a tiny boat made from a pandanus leaf and a stick. I wondered what people believed in and held to in purgatory, what they hoped for, looked forward to each day.

One man had his shirt off, a towel around his neck like a boxer. Crosshatched suture scars ran under under his arms, the skin drawn in tight where his nipples and lymph nodes had been removed. Each time he raised his arms to clap, the towel wagged across his chest.

Cardboard posters with the names of islands where people were from had been tacked to the outside of the building: Rongelap, Utirik, Namu, Wotje, Likiep, some islands directly downwind from the tests. In the future there would be American posters up to announce U.S. compensation to islanders for radiation-related medical problems: the dollar value on their thyroids, cancer, stillbirths, heart disease, retardation, deaths.

At the end of the dance a man in a root beer–colored shirt blared through a bullhorn and waved his arm for people to get out. Dancers began clearing from the church. The tape player stopped, and the crowd looked around, murmuring. I watched for May and Libby, but I didn't know what I'd do if I saw them.

Someone started yelling, pointing down the road. Five men were carrying what I thought at first was a crucifix. They moved closer, slowly. On their shoulders was a crude six-foot-long plywood model of a plane fuselage, the wings off it. Behind them two gray-haired men carried the wings under their arms like surfboards.

People gathered around as the group took the model into the church. I watched from the window. The two older men set the wings on the church floor and then helped the others lift the plane up high to hook on to a wire, running the length of the room. The fuselage swayed on the line. Someone had shellacked the whole model, bringing up the honey color of the watery grain. The plane windshield was painted blue. Three of the men assembled the roughly cut wings into notches on the fuselage.

Music started up again, and a group of dancers practiced in place outside as they waited. I noticed Ray moving through the crowd, carrying two styrofoam cups in his hands, looking around. He stepped alongside a girl at the end of the line of dancers. With his arms raised, the drinks up high, he began trying to dance with the teenagers.

His yellow polo shirt was damp from sweat. I could see that as he got closer. I could see his face, tanned and leathery, his gray eyes. When he saw me, he came over and pushed one of the drinks into my hand. He grabbed my arm and tried to pull me out. "You could use a dance," he yelled out. "It's Christmas."

Some poor dumb bastard who didn't know what he'd walked into. "There's no dance, for Godsake," I shouted back at him. "Get out of there." I moved away and tried to get lost in the crowd.

The Marshallese men were fussing with the underside of the plane as it rocked on the wire. The smell of lighter fluid tanged the room. One of the men working on the plane yelled out, and someone stopped the tape player again. The lights were flipped off; the church went dark. People whispered and laughed, trying to find one another.

With no announcement, two men at the plane pushed it down the wire just as a third man struck a match to the bottom of the model. The men jumped back. A sizzling sound, then a ball of fire ballooned from the fuselage in a small explosion. People screamed. A metal plate on the bottom of the plane slammed off and scratched across the concrete floor. Out of the fuselage a large cylinder dropped and swung on the end of a rope.

The heavy plane still scraped down the wire, straining in slow jerks. A little retarded girl was curled up on the ground, crying from the noise. Lights went up in the church.

Dangling from the plane was a "nuclear bomb," whittled from wood and painted silver. On it a small artificial Christmas tree swayed, dollar bills clipped to the green, frilled limbs. Quarters were still spilling out of the fuselage, along with candy, glitter, and confetti. Small bars of soap, packs of ramen, pink and blue vegetable-dyed baking flour in Baggies had dropped from the cavity.

A man blasted through the bullhorn again. Children ran out on the floor, yelling, gathering up the candy, throwing it at one another. Music on the tape player started up, and the dancers began stomping through the cellophane bags of noodles, the coins, candy.

I watched the islanders lost from their lives for a few hours. A gray-haired man plucked a dollar bill from the tree. The bomb turned on its rope, the money tree bobbling off it. Kids scrambled on the floor. The audience darted in to retrieve the gifts of the appalling piñata.

I could have added to the eerie celebration with confetti of bone, burned salt. If I'd poured the ash into a pair of pants and shirt and knotted the ends, Beebe and I would have been the ones to dance. Later, I could have unknotted a leg and drawn out a generic outline of a body, caught in a last pose, chalked in at the scene of the crime.

I would never make sense of the ironies in this place that made no sense. One irony was that Micronesia had been a Trust Territory since 1947. The U.S. had been entrusted to safeguard the health and welfare of the people.

"You don't know the Marshallese and what's hap- pened," Beebe had always told me. "Maybe you had a crush on a Marshallese boy from Ebeye. And you saw the radiation victims from Rongelap and Utirik up close. But you didn't know the language. You couldn't begin to understand their lives, what they'd gone through."

I didn't have the luxury now to get mad at Beebe for dismissing me. And he was right. What did I know really about the Marshallese? Strangers, unwilling travelers, picked up on the road in one of America's blackouts.

The next day, Christmas, I went to see May and Libby at Beebe's. Bougainvillea blazed over his cement-block house, the purple blossoms so brilliant they looked lumines- cent.

May's gray hair was up in a comb Beebe had given her on Kili. We sat at the kitchen table, Libby next to her mother. Beebe's features in Libby's face, the flat shape of her lips, the angle of her cheek and jaw, her eyes.

May put her hand over the top of the box when I brought it out of my bag. I tried to explain that he wanted his ashes divided.

May gasped something. Libby translated for her mother, tightness in her throat. "A man cannot be in parts. You cannot divide a man."

I suddenly saw the insult, the flippancy of his request. It had been only dark humor to him, but for them, death called for reverence, honoring.

The room was hot. I just wanted to go, take the ashes and leave, not put them through this.

May raised up the box, looking under it as if Beebe would somehow appear. On Kili he had brought May and Libby gifts. In 1954 I'd watched him open a box not too different from this one, but it held a pair of black-patent leather shoes for Libby.

That time on Kili in 1954, I saw Beebe go into May's thatched hut. I watched him cover her and Libby with a sheet as they lay still to sleep. From outside, I stared at the scene in the room lit by a kerosene lamp, saw into his parallel life—his transgressions, his attempted compensations, how far removed he was from me. He was tied to the islands, to the Marshallese through his daughter, to the unforgivable consequences of an era.

Now this day, Christmas, we would take all that was left over to Enubuj. Libby, May, and I in a boat. Libby gave me one of her *niqniqs,* a long dress, to wear for modesty.

By the islet we began wading out in the gowns. Libby was holding the container.

We all stepped into deeper water, up to our waists. Libby unfolded the plastic bag from the box and widened the opening.

In a year five hundred Marshallese landowners would sail out into this restricted zone, in spite of the incoming missiles from California. The islanders would try to reclaim the lagoon and the necklace of land in their atoll. They would set up camps on Kwaj next to the tennis courts. Rebellions in an occupied land. The Marshall Islands Constitution would go into effect in 1979, but the Marshallese would still not be disentangled from U.S. control.

Libby and I swam out farther and treaded water. She turned with the box toward the western and then the eastern chain of atolls that makes up the Marshalls: *Ralik*—"toward sunset," *Ratak*—"toward sunrise." Fish bumped us and swam in closer, opening their mouths. Beebe caught in our hair, in the dresses, swelling in the current.

Between Territories

When my mother, Matty, was expected to die, she had a talk with the dead and went to the past to mend something.

"It's like it's 1918 again," she told me. "The sounds after the First War. Firecrackers, guns going off in the woods. Everything larger than life, they said."

"They" were dead family members. "The contacts" she called them. My mother stretched out her fingers to her unseen mother, Josephine, then drew back her hand, holding what she said were red clay marbles rolled from dirt where she'd grown up.

With her other hand Matty grabbed my arm. "I'll be out of this used-up bag. Life is a human joke."

I swiped the air around the hospital bed. As much as I wanted to believe that the dead were there and the cool air I moved through was my family, I was afraid. They were a sign of Matty's leaving. I told them to get out.

★   ★   ★

It was 1989, San Diego, years since we'd lived in the Trust Territory of the Pacific Islands, miles away. But now it was our turn to be betrayed. Doctors from Matty's health maintenance organization had failed to provide necessary tests to diagnose and treat her heart disease over the last two years, had mistaken congestive heart failure for an "ear infection" and sent her home. The cost of medical tests came out of doctors' salaries, but we didn't know that then.

Later in the hospital Matty would go into a coma. The doctors would call it hopeless and would urge that tube feeding not be continued.

But Matty wouldn't die, even without nutrition. She would survive a six-week euthanasia effort and regain consciousness after I went against all the doctors' advice. She'd come back changed from something I didn't understand.

"They're standing right there, saying if I'm not happy in a life, I have a right to dissolve it," Matty said. No one else was with us. Four days later she'd go into a coma.

"I have until Friday to decide, they said. I'm writing all about 1935 now," the year she was married. But she was too sick even to hold a pen, and doctors told me there was brain impairment.

"Nineteen thirty-five, Lee," she insisted. "I'm there."

Matty patted the hospital bed, her fragile arm moving through the air as if the air had weight, her face delicate with high cheekbones. She'd always been beautiful, but she never acknowledged it.

"Come lie down next to your mama." Her fingers with marble-size joints from arthritis, calloused from hard work all her life. She'd been a seamstress for other people, ripping out seams; stitching blouses, coats; running up the sides of dresses on her sewing machine; down on her knees marking hems. With pins in her mouth, Matty would go on about the lack of quality in anything store-bought: no linings; crooked, chintzy seams. She'd rip out her own work and redo it until it was perfect. When I was growing up, she made all my clothes, instructing me later about the soft lines of silk, the tastefulness of a camel's-hair coat, the integrity of lined pockets.

I lay down on the edge of the hospital bed next to Matty. I had lain next to her the night we found out my brother, Jim, had died. I woke that morning after his death to find Matty studying me, her hand just above my face.

Now I tried to remember everything my mother ever taught me about death. Years before, she'd laughed telling the story of the family laying out Grandmother Mary on the parlor table after she'd died, and the old lady's cheeks sunken from lack of teeth. Someone went to get a wad of sheep's wool, and they plumped up the old woman's mouth, giving her a face she hadn't had in years.

When someone in the family was about to die, Mary came to them, patting her sheep wool cheeks in jest and offering her hand for the crossing. In dreams, relatives saw her holding dead family members as infants again, cradled as they'd never been in their real lives.

There were other Ozark stories. A mother from a nearby farm couldn't accept the death of her son. He had left a note: "I have gone to meet the train." Then he lay down on the tracks. She kept his last dinner plate just as he'd left it, with scraps of ham and sweet potato, preserved under a glaze of clear varnish.

On a farm death was matter-of-fact. The quick snap of a duck's neck in your hands, hogs butchered each winter.

"They said you're in danger, not ready. I can't leave yet," Matty told me in the hospital.

I touched my mother's blue cotton hospital gown, laid my hand over her chest. I could feel the breastbone, fragile as a bird's. Her enlarged heart moved in its jerky rhythm. A doctor had called her heart function "incompatible with life."

"Look at Jim," Matty said. "He's smiling. He's gone on, done more work. Death is no failure."

I couldn't see my brother. Since he'd committed suicide ten years before, I'd imagined him traveling rapidly away as sound through outer space.

He'd been a biophysicist doing research in genetics and alcoholism, working with alcoholic lab mice that binged all day, sousing themselves by inhaling alcohol up their snouts. "Most of the offspring end up alkies," he had told me. "Don't let your genes take over, Lee." He knew it in himself.

A scientist to the end, he'd detailed the sensations as he died, the effects of what he'd taken, noting exact times.

"Things couldn't be any better," Jim had said the last time I talked to him. He'd already made his plan. Over the phone I had even called him Bubba again, although we hadn't called him that in years.

After his death, I stood out in the backcountry of San Diego, raging at him for what he'd done. I was kicking a boulder, took off my jacket and whipped it against the rock when I noticed a Mexican national in the bushes, trying to get across the border. He must have been amazed at an American who was supposed to have everything, but was *loco* in the *cabeza*. A border-patrol plane flew overhead, and the man crawled under my car to hide. Surviving day to day is all most people can ever afford.

"You see Jim there?" Matty said to me now. "Look at him. He wasn't afraid to go."

★ ★ ★

The next day Matty went into a coma. I lay next to her in nights to come, holding her hand, as if I could anchor her to life, trying to make up for the times I hadn't appreciated her, had walled her off.

On the third morning she rallied. She opened her eyes, taking time to focus, then began speaking softly. "I'm leaving this territory. I'll be gone by the end of the day. It's time." She smoothed the sheet by her side.

"Don't even think it," I said. "I'll bring you home and take care of you."

"I'll be the one coming to you, Lee. Sit quiet anywhere. Don't be afraid."

We were talking about two different things, the territory of life and the one of death.

I went to get my father and brought him to the hospital to say good-bye to her. He sat down in a chair next to the bed and asked her when she was coming home, told her how he'd cleaned the house that day.

"Tell her how you feel about her," I said. "She has to know."

He started about the war years together, the destroyer he'd been on. "Goddammit, didn't know if I'd live or die. Men dropping like flies on the deck. A picture of my family around the Christmas tree, banging against my bunk when the Japs torpedoed. Now we're making them rich buying their goddamn cars."

Matty opened her eyes, looked at him, shaking her head, and then closed her lids again.

He stood up from the chair and stumbled against it. He was bleary-eyed, thin, unsteady from drinking.

"We want you to get well, Mama," I told her.

"Maybe we'll all get well. All of us." She didn't look at Jack and me.

"We thought we were all going to die in that tidal wave on Kwaj," my father tried again. "Remember, Matty, old girl?" He cracked mints in his mouth and tried to laugh, reaching over to grab her shoulder lightly and shaking it, as if he expected her to snap out of this dying.

We looked at her with her eyes closed, mouth parted, and I imagined we both thought then that this was how she'd look when life was gone. I motioned toward her, for my father to say something more.

"I've seen too much death," Jack said suddenly. "Shipmates burned to ash and hosed out of the boiler room during the war. I don't let it get to me anymore." His head moved unsteadily.

"This is your wife," I said. "It's Mama."

"Say another word and I'll shoot you. I've got enough problems without you." He glared at me. "I'm talking, goddammit. The commanding officer. *Achtung!*"

To sit here in this tiny room with the same phrases we'd heard all the years. Both of them furious at their lives.

"Fifty-three years of marriage." Jack grabbed the side railing of the bed and rattled it. "Just a poor old broken-down sailor without a wife now. Fifty-three years."

With her eyes closed, Matty raised her head slightly off the pillow. "Till death do us part. And that's it. You hear me?" She settled back. By evening she'd returned to the coma.

It was before and after Matty's coma that they came through scenes, lore, details of the hardness of their lives, choices made in lives that weren't part of them now. My brother, Jim; Matty's mother, Josephine. Mary, the grandmother.

"In the full picture," Matty said before the coma, "Josephine gives me the bead necklace."

One time when Matty was four, her father gave her a gift of beads painted gold. "That ain't necessary," Josephine said, taking them off her. "No one gets special fussing."

People just endured. Josephine was a black-haired girl once who rode sidesaddle to town in a brown serge skirt to have her teeth pulled out in the barbershop. She crunched across molars on the barber's floor in her ill-fitting Sears shoes stuffed with newspaper.

Pregnant at fifteen and every other year for the next twenty-eight, fourteen children. Even the country doctor said for Godsake, let me do something to stop this. Josephine turned her face to the floral sprigs on the wallpaper, the hand prints burnished into the wrought-iron headstead, and pretended she didn't hear.

"Kids just didn't have value," Matty had said to me years before. "Kept my eyes crossed all day once, and no one even noticed."

It meant something peculiar in the back hills of the Ozarks when Matty was born tiny enough to fit in a shoe box but had a full head of red hair and long fingernails. Each baby was wrapped in red flannel to bring out the hives, but Matty came at the world like a hornet with singed wings.

"I always told everyone exactly what I thought," Matty said to me once. "Every blessed one of them. Even the boy Jesus threw pinecones at his playmates. I'm sure he did."

Some of the stories I'd heard and could give detail to. "It would begin," Matty said, pausing. "I'd go someplace where I could be alone. Walk into hollyhocks over my head, curtains of stalks, the worm-eaten leaves like lace gloves gently touching on my back. I'd hide in the dirt there where no one could know me."

Josephine was running to the smokehouse with kids grabbing on to her skirt. She held up a bottle of iodine in her hand, waving it in an arc as if selling a potion. "I'm going to swaller i-o-dean if you don't leave me alone. You wait and see. Get a moment's peace if I have to be stone dead."

The whole place in an uproar until the old man was called in from the field to yell sense into her and those kids.

"He acted like he was God," Matty told me. "Railing against all of us as sinners, the whole county sinners going to burn in the flames of hell. I hated God for years because of him. I'd leave that place. Go where no one could find me. Into the woods to lie under a blanket of dried blond pine needles. The whole damn mess could be gone, vanished."

All day Josephine wore the splattered muslim blouse with iodine bled deep in the coarse weave. The kids were silent. The only sound was the pop of June bugs on the porch. Smell of the woody river and rain coming. Josephine held a woven straw fan up to her face to stir the air in the humid summer heat. Her splashed hands kept them in fear, waving back and forth, back and forth.

"In the full picture," Matty said now, "Josephine whisks the fan over me. It's redone. She gives me the necklace."

In the hospital I waited for Matty's death. She wasn't dying. I wrote questions to ask doctors. I've had waiters in restaurants take more time describing a dessert tray than they took to answer. I would be selfish to keep her alive, I was told. She had a living will, stating she didn't want to be prolonged if death was imminent. But days were going to weeks as she survived on only IV fluids. She was moved to a convalescent home to die.

Matty was going through levels of starvation, as shocking in appearance as a concentration camp victim. Sharp outlines of ribs, collarbone, shoulders. Deeply sculpted thighs and stomach contrasted with the startling jut of hipbones. I could see the motion of her large heart against tissue skin.

We finally obtained regular heath insurance. I was questioning if the right to die had been abused in the rationed-care HMO system, if Matty had been written off too quickly. I discussed tube feeding with Hospice, with other doctors who wouldn't question their colleagues. Let your mother go. She's made it to her seventies; she's had a long life.

My father blocked an attempt I made to start tube feeding. He was in a blackout of advanced alcoholism. The following day he had forgotten what he'd done.

I requested tube feeding again later. The doctor tried to talk me out of it. "Do you believe in God?" he asked.

"I don't know."

"Do you believe in nature? If nature had wanted your mother to eat, she'd be eating." Then he had the head of the convalescent home speak to me.

I went back to Matty's room. I decided I would act out feeding her. My mother, who had kept everyone fed, always in the process of preparing meals, dinner on the table every night at six.

I held an eyedropper of nutrition drink up to her mouth. There was a streak of red in her gray hair that hadn't been red in years, a sign of starvation. "Let me feed you, Mama. Don't die."

I touched the creamy fluid to her lips, pretending I was feeding her, doing what hadn't been done. She was my daughter now.

She left the Ozarks on Greyhound, headed for San Diego with a paper bag of her things. Nineteen thirty-five. An amber bead necklace a brother had brought back from the Orient, safety-pinned to a slip strap she kept checking every few minutes the whole trip. The beads deep red amber, the color of her hair.

In a photo album I had, Matty stood before a black DeSoto Airflow near a gumdrop bungalow in San Diego. A cluster of banana trees with dwarf bananas stood in the courtyard.

In the album were old postcards—grainy, brightly colored pictures of the 1935 Pacific Expo in Balboa Park. Hollywoodland lights on the reflecting pools of water lilies. The "nudist" colony on the midway. Viny gardens out of Maxfield Parrish paintings. "Fleet Week," with 114 warships in the harbor. On the front of that card someone had drawn in fountain pen an arrow pointing to one of the ships and "Here I am, your fellow in whites."

I found the little cottage where Matty had lived in 1935. In the courtyard were the banana trees with bright green leaves. The places were vacant, but Matty was here reliving 1935. I watched for her to come home from her job at Woolworth's, the bookbindery, or the dress shop where she alters clothes. She'd wear a long skirt, flowered peplum, maybe a necklace she'd strung with hard macaroni dyed blue and green. High heels on, rayon stockings, her legs thin from not enough to eat back home.

Matty will come home on the streetcar, carrying a chop wrapped in white paper from the butcher shop. She'll leave for the evening with a sailor to dance at Lubach's. Jack, handsome and snappy in his sailor whites.

I'll stop her at the gate when she comes home and tell her what was ahead. I wouldn't be someone she would even talk to if I weren't her daughter now.

"Who are you? Get out of my way, sister," she'd tell me.

She wore a dark blue dress to be married in at the justice of the peace. The amber necklace with the tiny insects suspended in the beads. A corsage of forget-me-nots. A few minutes in a ceremony that will tie people to a lifetime.

I went another time to the cottage and looked into the window. Inside was a built-in ironing board where she must have ironed her blue dress for her wedding, clothes for work. On the stove, a coffeepot boiled on the morning glory blue flame. Matty stooped over the radiator and dressed, the bumps of her spine showing through her nightgown. At night she stood at the kitchen window, shirt sleeves rolled up to her elbows as she split the seams of pea pods. In the window, her striking face: two streaks of rouge, the deep red bee-stung lips, eyebrows darkened with brown coloring pencil she'd wet with her tongue.

The light bulb dimmed, and the kitchenette yellowed. Rising in water running in the sink, a plum-colored kimono with a print of white chrysanthemums that Jack had bought. Matty looked out the back window to exotic fruit in someone's yard—avocados, lemons hanging like small golden lanterns in the trees. California, where no one knew her. Back home was the steady coil of dirt turned by horse-driven plow. Her old man farming the practical crops in ordered rows. Dogwood in the forest, the sight of a cardinal. There was comfort in the certain things of nature when you had nothing.

She remembered the one surprise of a piano hauled out to the farm by wagon. But the ropes broke, and the piano toppled, banging over the country road. All things taken from you. The keys would never be fixed, forever playing some quirky chords.

★ ★ ★

In the convalescent hospital Matty came back up as if from the depths of a deep pool. I had finally risked my own judgment, ignored doctors, and ordered tube feeding at six and a half weeks of the euthanasia effort. Within twelve hours Matty was talking. In a few days she was humming along with Christmas carols.

"This is earth," she said a week later. "I wouldn't go with them." She waved a hand dismissively. "I told them to forget it."

"I'll be writing about what you went through with the medical care," I told her.

"Be aggressive. I want to be whatever help I can." Matty reached for my hand and then, with it, moved as if to music. "What can we have for lunch that would be some great delicacy? An avocado?"

She wrote her name soon after that, the feeding tube was removed in a month, and she began to eat on her own. A little later, Matty started to walk with assistance. Sitting down to rest one time, she put her legs in the air, pedaling them to get stronger.

"The lazy lizard is rising up, becoming more powerful," she told me that day. Then she wrote on a pad of paper: "I use my abilities. Chosen to live my own way."

Two years later there was a House subcommittee investigation into Medicare's failure to protect seniors from the medical abuses in Medicare HMOs. News shows did exposés about managed care putting profit before lives. In 1992, *60 Minutes* investigated the Medical Board of California and its refusal to regulate negligent and incompetent doctors. I tried to make sense of what had occurred. Why things had happened the way they did.

I took care of Matty at my house. Once we went back to their home, where Jack still lived. I moved Matty around the yard in her wheelchair, and she called out names of flowers: cosmos, sweet William, jasmine. Some of them were wrong. "Bleeding heart" she called camellia.

Matty picked an orange from one of her trees. She bit back the skin and spit out the tart fruit. The juice dripped over her spindly fingers. E.T. hands she called them, looking down, turning them. "My God, look at those hands," as if they didn't belong to her anymore. She tossed the orange into the dirt.

"Can we make it?" I asked Matty that day. I didn't know if we could get by.

"We're going to make it," Matty said. "Sure we can. Don't doubt."

Years before, she had told me the story about a Fourth of July after the First World War. "A hundred pound block of ice came up on the Frisco train," she had said. "We met it at the whistle stop in a wagon. Wrapped it up in a quilt to take back and make ice cream. Everyone was looking forward to it for months. The only thing we had. But something went wrong. Salt got in the cream. Someone had to plug up the hole in the ice-cream maker with an old cotton stocking. You made do in those days. We ate salty ice with cream anyway." Matty had smiled when she told the story then. She was still lovely now but very frail because of the unnecessary physical suffering of the last years.

"You're different, Lee," she told me in the yard. "You've changed. You're a more giving person, closer to me."

I would never be the same. I'd learned once more never to relinquish my thinking to anyone. I'd also fallen completely in love with Matty.

Her eyes now were beginning to look unfocused into another place. "Little assaults on the brain, lack of oxygen because of her heart," a doctor had said.

But this day we watched a bird gulping down orange berries from a pyracantha.

In a month Matty would be leaving. Into the hollyhocks in her blue dress, amber beads. The gloves taking her in, bringing her back.

"Mind always goes on," Matty told me. "As real as breathing and digesting. No convoluted religion. Nothing mysterious."

A week after my mother died, my father had his military uniform dry cleaned, medals polished and repinned, ready for his burial. It was as if he were still in the military and had gotten orders, hurried up to go, and then had been left waiting.

He typed out his obituary, naming all the wars that spanned his years, starting from when he was a small child during World War I and saw the doughboys going off. As the soldiers waited for the trains that would take them away, they tossed him up on a blanket, yelling "Hip, hip, hoorah" and singing "For He's a Jolly Good Fellow." The exhilaration he felt as he went higher. I don't know how far back I would have to go to find that boy, so bright, never envisioning his life like this.

At the end, when my father was as fragile as an infant, he asked me, "Where's Matty? What ever happened to Jim?" He held my hand tightly in his.

And when he was gone, I thought he'd probably left the way we had always traveled. He'd be up by four in the morning, anxious to get on the road and get where we were going. We'd pull out of an auto court by four-fifteen and he'd hit the gas, floor it, crackling gravel under the tires. "Thank God we got the hell out of there," he'd bellow.

I go to the park where my parents used to take walks through the eucalyptus trees, people who may never have belonged together, but I imagine them still walking there and what it would be like if things had been different.

In the full picture my mother is sewing back at home, holding a needle up and drawing thread through it. The methodical hand-stitches in the clothes are even, durable, as they always have been. There is an unfinished oil painting of a Siberian tiger she'll come back to paint. In the dark out back, my brother sights the moon through a telescope as I stand beside him. And through the night my father reads about the precarious course of history.